Joseph

BENTLEY LEGACY BOOK 2

KATHI S. BARTON

World Castle Publishing, LLC
Pensacola, Florida

Copyright © Kathi S. Barton 2015
Hardback ISBN: 9781629893044
Print ISBN: 9781629893051
eBook ISBN: 9781629893068
First Edition World Castle Publishing, LLC, July 24, 2015
http://www.worldcastlepublishing.com

Cover: Karen Fuller
Editor: Eric Johnston
Editor: Maxine Bringenberg

Chapter 1

Chris wasn't sure what to think. She'd been trying to find this Bentley person for a month now, and all she'd been able to find was a big fat nothing. Glaring at the list of names that her secretary had found for her, she wondered, not for the first time, why her older sister had been killed.

Chris turned just as someone came into her office. She did not want to deal with Jackson today.

"Miss McKenzie, I have a message from the billing department that says that you're not turning in all your hours. Is that true?" Chris sat at her desk, calming herself before she flew across the room and murdered him. "You know that we only get paid when you bill the correct amount of time?"

"I'm well aware of how billing works, Jackson. I have worked here longer than you have. And why are they telling you my business?" When he sat down, she groaned. "Don't you have something else to do? Like push little old men under buses? I've heard that you might be pretty good at that."

It was a rumor, of course, that he'd gotten his job because someone in the firm had been killed by a bus. Everyone, her included, thought he'd done it. He and this other man, Jim Carter, had been in the running for the partnership, and he'd just eliminated his competition. The longer Chris knew Jackson Hill, the more she thought him capable of just about anything.

"I've already turned in my hours for the week." Chris glanced at her calendar and saw that it was only Thursday. "I know what you're thinking. But it's fine. I've talked to Duncan and he said that if my hours went over, I'd have to eat them. They won't."

"And if they go under?" He snorted at her. "Whatever, Jackson. I have work to do and it's not getting done with you in here. So move it. Go to your own part of the building and leave me to mine."

He took his time standing up, and she noticed that he was staring at her desk like he was trying to memorize it. She knew what he could see. Nothing. Her desk was covered in paperwork, both business and personal, but all he could see was what she let him. A neat, clean desk with thick folders labeled with numbers.

"You're entirely too secretive, love. Why don't you trust me?" Chris leaned back in her chair and said nothing. "Why don't you and I have dinner tonight? We could go over some of the questions you might have about my personal life, and then we could go back to your place for a night of great sex."

"Never going to happen, Jackson." He asked her why. "Because I don't like you. I doubt that having sex with you would improve my opinion of you. And, as it happens, I have a date."

"Do you now? With who? Someone I know? No, that's not possible. Everyone I know would never encroach on you. They know that as my partner in this firm, you belong to me." Chris stood up and was glad that he took several steps back. "I'm kidding you, love. I've never said a word about us."

Chris was furious, but she pointed to the door rather than direct her magic to him. It would have been hard to explain, and she was much too busy right now to try to placate anyone that would care to inquire as to why he was dead. Chris doubted that anyone would care a button, and they'd more than likely give her a medal for it.

When he left her office, she closed the door using just a bit of her magic and stared at her desk. Where was this man, and why had Angel thought he could help Chris? Picking up the list that she'd been working on, she called the next name. All the Bentleys that she'd managed to eliminate had been marked through, and there were only about two dozen of them left. Who knew there could be so many of them all over the United States, and not a one of them with the name Micah?

"Hello, I'm looking for a man by the name of Micah Bentley." The sound coming through the phone was like a low growl. "My name is Chris."

"He's probably working." Her heart started to pound in her chest. "I don't think he's supposed to be back before...I don't even...do you know what time it is, lady?"

She glanced at her computer, then at the number. It was three hours earlier in the man's house. Telling him she was sorry, Chris heard the man—because there was no doubt that was what it was on the other end—laugh.

"Look, it's okay. I have to get up anyway in about two hours. Micah is...he has his own home now. I can give you…no, that will only piss him off. Give me your number and I'll have him call you." Chris gave him both her personal number and her office number. "He might not call you right away. I think one of his daughters was sick last night and they were up. He called me about three to— yeah, like you're interested in that."

"I just need him to answer a few questions for me. Tell him it's about my sister, Angel." The silence at the other end had her standing up. Chris had no idea what was going through the man's head, but she knew that he'd heard of Angel and more than likely knew what might have happened to her. "She told me before she died to contact him and that he'd have some answers for me."

"Micah said to give you his number." His voice was no longer sexy sounding. Now it was hard, almost like he was pissed at her. "He asked that you wait five minutes before you call. He wants to get in the shower to wake up."

"All right."

The line went dead. The deep silence on the line made her think that had it been a house phone, one that actually hung up. She thought she might have heard the sound of it as it vibrated though her head when he'd slammed it down. Putting down her phone, she sat there and stared at the clock across the room on her wall.

The short burst of someone knocking was all the warning she got before her dad walked in. He was a partner at Roger, Roger, and Rocklin too, but few people knew they were related. Her dad's last name was different than hers because he was her stepfather, and few knew that. When Allen Black sat down, he frowned.

"What is it? Did you hear what Jackson is telling people?" Chris asked him what he'd said. "The moron is saying that you need your space today. He thinks you might be a little menstrual. I hope his dick falls off."

Chris really didn't like the guy before, and now she really hated him. "Next time you see him, tell him that he's on my list. He asked me to have dinner with him tonight and then we'd go to my house for sex."

"Good God." Chris laughed, then glanced at the clock again. "I'm sorry, am I bothering you? You've looked at the time a lot since I came in."

"No. I got a lead on this Bentley guy." Dad leaned forward and asked her in a low voice what it was. "I have to call him back. In two minutes. Would you like to be here?"

"Yes, if you don't mind." Chris knew that even though he was their stepfather, Allen loved them as much or more than their own father might have. And when Angel's body had come to her, he was with her. They were moving her things from her apartment to his house in an effort to consolidate their money right now.

When it was time, Chris picked up the phone and called Micah. Her hands were sweaty and her head was pounding. After the fourth ring she nearly hung up, but a woman answered and she was laughing.

"He wants to know if you set a timer." Chris didn't know what to say so said nothing to the still laughing woman. "His mom is coming to help out, so just hang on a bit. Micah said he's about done."

The phone was set down, and that was when she heard the child howling. And when it was abruptly cut off, Chris could imagine that a bottle had been put in the child's mouth to shut it up. The laughing woman was talking to someone else, and that was when she heard who she would bet was Micah talking.

"I know what I said. And I'm going to do it, just not as quickly as I said I would." He didn't sound the least bit repentant of whatever it was he was supposed to be doing. "I've been a little busy, in case you hadn't noticed."

"Oh, I noticed. You're very busy playing with that new system you got for your birthday, and building that playhouse for the girls. You do know that it's going to be a few years before they can even walk to it, much less play with it, right?" The woman squealed and Chris smiled. "Stop it. Stop right now before I tell your mother."

The laughter continued until the phone was dropped. Then the man that she knew was going to give her some answers answered the phone. Chris felt her eyes fill as emotion, stronger than anything she'd ever felt before, took her breath away. Her dad took the phone.

~~~

Micah said hello again before someone finally answered him. He'd been expecting a woman's voice and was thrown off when a man spoke. But he explained quickly who he was and why it was him talking to him instead of Chris.

"As you can imagine, we're all very broken up over the death of Angel. She'd been away for a while, yes, but she was due to come home to us soon. You were the last person to see her." Micah pointed out that he'd been one of the last people to see her, as he'd not killed her. "Yes, that's right. Her body came to us just moments after her...we'd like to talk to you. Person to person if you can manage it."

"I can't right now. I'm a new father and we're trying to get our lives figured out." Micah looked over at Reggie as she fed Alexis her bottle. Mom was feeding Anne and he felt his heart swell with love for them all. "I don't know where you are, but if you were to see your way here, I'd

10

make sure you had everything you needed. Angel...she saved my life, I think."

"I would say that she did from the look of things." Micah had gone back to the scene with Joey that day. There was nothing there. No body, no blood, and his clothing had been taken away, along with everything in the office where he'd been talking to Angel. Even her car, the one that she'd been about to drive off in, was gone. "Do you know what she was? My daughter, did she tell you what she was?"

"No. I saw her and her sigil. I've tried to figure out what it was, but there is nothing that I can see. She let down her guard at one point, but all I saw was that she was brilliantly white and that she was dressed in a kind of armor. To be honest with you, I've begun to doubt my sanity lately over this. It's as if...well, it's been very odd."

"Odd how?" Micah watched his daughter and wife as he thought of the man's question. But before he could form an answer, even if he had one, the man spoke. "I'm not sure how long it will be before we can come to you. I'm not sure where you are, but I think Chris knows. Perhaps you can give us a few days to sort out our end. Things are a little...a little tight here, and we have to see what we can do."

"I can send a plane for you." The man said nothing, and Micah felt like this was the right thing to do. "Just tell me when and where, and I'll have it there for you. You can stay here too. The house is big enough for guests, and you won't have to worry about that either."

"That's very generous of you, Mr. Bentley, but we can't put you out." Micah assured him that they wouldn't be. "I'll talk to my daughter and get back with you then. I don't mind telling you that this is a great gift you've given us. As I said, things have been a little tight around here lately, and we're trying to recoup our losses."

After he hung up, only just then realizing that not only hadn't he gotten the man's name but still had no idea what Angel had been, his mom handed him the now sleeping Anne. He looked at Reggie when she said his name.

"What do you think?"

"What?"

"I don't know, this and that. Inviting them here. Do you think that's a good idea? I mean, for all we know they could be mass murderers and kill us in our sleep."

"They could be, but I'm pretty sure that our being panthers would win over a mass murderer. And you have to stop watching that stupid station. Mom is as bad as you are about doom and death." She giggled and kissed the top of Alexis's head before standing up to take her to the bed. He followed and was disappointed that he'd not been able to feed at least one of them. It was what he looked forward to all day, holding them while they ate. "As for inviting them to stay here, I don't know why but I feel like I can trust them. Angel was…there was something about her that made me feel like she was telling me the truth."

And Angel had been right about the others too. Sadie Greer—otherwise known by any of a dozen other names such as Maggie Sands, Sandy Woods, and the list went on—had been the second in command to a large money laundering operation. Her partner, Sam Sandalwood, also with an impressive list of aliases, had been arrested with her. But things had happened at the station where they'd been held.

"When do you think they'll be here?" Micah pulled Reggie into his arms and told her he didn't know. "But you feel this is the thing to do? Do you think it will help you with the nightmares? Maybe they can shed some light on them."

"I don't know." The nightmares had been horrific, some so bad that he'd woken up screaming. He never knew what they had been about when he woke, and no matter how hard he tried, he couldn't go back to sleep afterwards. And the effects of it were hurting him, he knew it.

"Well, if you don't mind, I'd very much like to make this a family affair. Everyone here and staying here until they leave, or we find out they're all right." Micah thought it was a great idea and told her that. "Also, I'd like to ask you a favor. Not a big one, but still, I need it from you."

"Anything, you know that. All you have to do is ask and it's—" Reggie put her hand over his mouth and he grinned at her from behind it. He kissed her fingers and smiled at her.

"I don't want you to make promises like that. I've told you that before." He nodded, knowing that she'd have whatever she wanted. "But I need this. I want you to go out and help Joey. He's been asking for you to go to his place, and I also know that you're not going because of me. I can't, not yet."

"I know, love. And it's not just because of you that I haven't been out there, it's everything. I worry about you and the girls. I hate leaving you alone." She snorted. "Okay, so you're here with everyone else, but I still worry."

"Just go. He needs you as much as I need you out of the house. Please? Besides, I'm going to the diner today. It's the grand-reopening next week, and I want to make sure that everyone is ready." Micah didn't point out that everyone was ready now, but nodded. "I'm nervous no one will show up, and what will those people do?"

"I doubt very much that no one will show. You've been badgering people for two weeks now about the opening and— Ouch! That hurt." She started to pinch him again, and he backed up. "Stop that. What are you trying to do, bruise my poor old body?"

"I have not badgered a single person. And I'll have you know that Jimmy is nervous too. The poor man called here twice yesterday because he couldn't remember something. He forgot how to turn on the grill, and then he called to ask me where the pancake recipe was. I tell you, he's going to have a stroke, and then where will I be?"

"You'd be right there cooking for him until he was better." He grabbed her hands when she reached for him again. "If you behave and let me leave here without another bruise, I'll go now. Joey is nervous too, and it's doubtful that you can take over for him. Plus, he has a big court thing going on tomorrow."

"I know he is nervous. He called here last night and talked to your grandda. I think he's headed out there as well. I understand that the barn shell is up, as well as they're starting on the inside of the house." Micah nodded. It was going to be a beautiful house. "And the horses, have they arrived yet?"

"Not yet. He would like for you to come out when he gets them." Reggie said she'd think about it. Micah knew that she was still hurting from what had happened at the property. She'd killed two men bent on killing her and his mom, and had she not done what she'd done, they'd both be dead now. As it was, Reggie wasn't able to go there until Joey had his own house finished. "He got himself some barn kittens, as well as a dog."

"A dog?" He grinned and nodded. "What's going to happen with that? The poor thing is going to be confused every time he smells the cat in Joey."

"That's why he got him as a puppy. If he can get this to work for him, I think we should get a pup for the girls when they're old enough. They could have him to train and play with." She only patted him on the cheek as she walked away from him. Micah was having a blast being a dad.

The girls were mirror twins, born to a woman who had died moments before they'd been born and who had not been able to see her daughters or even to name them. Her husband and other family members had been killed immediately, and Micah's grandparents had contacted him to see if he and Reggie wanted to take them. Otherwise they would have been put into the system, and who knew what would have happened to them there?

He was nearly to his truck when Grandda came out of the house with a large box. Micah helped him load it in the back of his SUV and then waved goodbye to his grandma and mom as they watched them drive away. Micah looked over at his grandda as he just sat there, seemingly pissed off.

"Your grandmother is a pain in the ass." Micah laughed when Grandda looked around to see if he'd been overheard. "Well, she is. And if she was here, I'd tell her that. Did you know that she's got me on this diet? Why? I've lived a good long time without nobody telling me what to eat and not to eat."

"I'm sure she just wants you to live a little longer. Anne and Alexis would tell you the same thing if they could talk." Grandda looked at him with a twinkle in his eye. "You're not going to get anything out of me in the way of food either, so just back off. I've been given orders too. She said if she even smelled mustard on your breath, she was going to hang me out to dry. And don't even ask me what kind of mustard she's talking about. We're not going to the diner today."

"I just was helping out the man, that's all." Micah had heard the story. He and Jimmy had tried every recipe on the menu—all the pies, cakes, and other confections before starting on all the soups and sandwiches. By the time Grandma had gotten there to pick up Grandda, he'd been nearly sick he'd been so full. And they were complaining about the fact that they'd not gotten to the french fries and steaks as yet. "He wanted to make sure that he had them down pat before they opened."

"I'm pretty sure that had you just taken a taste of the things he offered you, it would have been fine. But I heard you'd eaten three banana pies yourself, as well as two cherry ones and three bowls of potato cheese soup, as well as five different subs." Grandda smiled at him. "That's not a good thing you did. You know that, right?"

"I know. But damn, it was fun. He kept telling me I was doing him a service. I gotta tell you that it's been a while since I've been a service for anyone." Micah knew the feeling. He'd been feeling a little left out himself lately. "I gotta find me a job, son. If I don't, I don't know what I'm going to do. The grandbabies are great, but they don't have it in them yet to go fishing and play some ball with this old man."

Micah decided to talk to the others. His grandda had been a cop, like his dad had been. And he was sure that had Dad not been killed so young, the two of them would have been having a grand old time with the babies. And if not for the fact that they couldn't hold a bottle, much less a pole, they'd be fishing with them too. Christ, Micah missed his dad right now.

"We'll think of something. And you coming out to Joey's with me, I do appreciate that. Reggie said you talked to him yesterday." He nodded. "Is he okay? The house is on schedule, right?"

"It is. A little ahead if you ask me, but he's…well, I'm thinking he's a tad lonely out there. He had Garth and Tony out the other day, and when they left he said the trailer he's staying in was just too quiet. I'm thinking I might stay with him a couple of days, see if I can get into some trouble with him." Grandda stiffened when he looked out the front window. "Holy Christ, he must be using magic to get this place done."

Micah looked out the window too. He'd been glancing at the gates when he went through them and didn't see the house at first. But he could see what Grandda was talking about. The house was framed in, the outside walls were up, and the porch, a huge wrap around, was having the railing put up. From where he sat, Micah thought the house looked finished. They both got out of the truck just as Joey came out of the house. He did not look happy.

Chapter 2

Joey greeted his brother with a nod because he could not get off the phone. The woman that he'd hired last week was going on and on about his appointments that he had missed. He tried to tell her three times that he'd had no appointments, and if he had them, she'd not told him.

"I do know what time I was coming into the office today. Four o'clock. I have several appointments to deal with, and then I'm going to stay in town to be there for my court appearance in the morning." She told him to hang on and put him on hold. Joey looked at Micah as he muted his phone. "I swear to Christ, I'm going to murder this woman. She's useless."

Joey wanted to quit his job. He'd been thinking about it for days now, and he was closer every minute to doing just that. He knew that he could open his own law firm and work on the cases that he wanted to work on, but the thought of being unemployed, even for the month it would take him to get set up, scared him shitless. It wasn't as if he couldn't afford to take the month off. He had a great deal of money, but he was afraid all the same. When he'd had enough of holding, he just ended the call and hugged his brother and grandda.

"You said yesterday that you had some stuff in the works. You still tossing that around?" Joey nodded at Grandda. He'd told him yesterday in a long call what he wanted to do. Grandda, of course, had supported him, even going so far as to tell him he'd help him out if he needed it. Joey told him he didn't need it but appreciated it. He'd yet to tell Micah.

The house was something that he could change the subject to, and he did it smoothly. There were still workers all over the house, most of them in his bedroom and the kitchen, but the rest of the house was coming along nicely too. There was a lot to do, but at the rate these guys were going, he'd be in the house in two weeks rather than two months. Joey was getting tired of the little trailer that he was currently staying in. He wished now that he'd not sold his house to Garth and had continued to live in it, instead of out here without much in the way of room.

They were coming down the stairs again when his phone rang. He was tempted to not answer it, but he did. As he made his way to his makeshift office, he told Micah to check out the back deck.

It was an hour before he got off the phone with the firm he worked for. And in the end, he had given his verbal notice to the partner that had called. It seemed that his secretary, Miss Gross, had gone to him complaining that her work was not appreciated. Paul Simmons had called to see what the problem was with her, not him.

"It's not working out." Paul told him he'd find him someone else. "No, I mean with me working all the time. The commute alone is about an hour one way. And my heart is no longer in it."

"We can't lose you, Joey. The firm needs good lawyers like you. Just let me find someone to replace her and we'll work this out. Hell, if you want to have Tabby for a while, I can spare her too. She's head over heels in love with you anyway. And if you want to work from home two or three days a week, I can live with that too. I need you. And Emmett will be so upset. I'll set things up for you."

Joey had felt like a large weight had been lifted from his shoulders when he actually said it and knew that there was no turning back. "I can't...I just can't do it. I love what I do, but I'm just exhausted with all this. I'm going to take some time off, finish my house, and raise some horses. I might put out my own shingle, but for now, I need to rest. I need this for me."

Paul told him he understood.

"You take some time off. We'll still be here when you come back. After a couple of months, if you still want to go down to part time, we'll work that out too. I really don't want to lose you." Joey thanked him but told him that he'd give him his resignation when he came in later. "I'll file it away for you. You can think about it. I'll let Emmett know, but I don't think he's going to be any happier about this than I am, okay?"

As far as Joey was concerned, he'd put more than enough thought into it already. As he sat there, trying to make his heart believe what his mouth had done, he smiled. For the first time in a long time, he felt like he was free.

Joey went to find his family. He found his brother in the kitchen on his cell, and Grandda was on the back deck. Joey went out there.

"Just beautiful here." Joey told him that he loved it. "That there lake, you gonna stock it? I have me a hankering to go get me a hook wet. I've been thinking about it since them little girls came into our lives."

"I never thought about it, but I think that's a great idea." Micah came out a few minutes later, just as Grandda was describing the boat that Joey should get to use, and he could tell that something had happened. "What is it, Micah? The girls? Mom or Reggie hurt?"

"No. I just got off the phone with a woman by the name of Chris McKenzie. I talked to her this morning after she called Garth by mistake. They're coming here." Joey nodded and held onto the railing that was still a little wobbly due to the fact that it was still being put in. "You remember her sister, Angel?"

"I do. What does she want? Did you tell her that you had nothing to do with the disappearance of her sister? Or anything else that happened that day?" Micah sat down on one of the large empty spools of wire that he'd been using as a table when he came out. "What is it, Micah?"

"She's coming here. Apparently...I guess when Angel died, her body went to them. I don't know how that worked yet, but I plan to have some answers. She's not upset, but she seems to think that her sister left her something with me. Did you see anything when I got to you?" Joey felt his heart tighten in his chest when he thought of how terrified he'd been when Micah had appeared before him naked and bloody. "I told her what I knew, but there was nothing else. She and her stepfather are going to come out here for a few days. She's a lawyer too, I guess."

"What do you suppose she wants? And why on earth are they coming here?" Grandda asked, and Joey was glad. He wanted to know as well but was still dealing with his own fears. "She's not thinking of suing you, is she? You tell her that you've done not a damned thing wrong."

"I did, and she's not worried about that. She's more concerned with her sister's legacy right now. I think…it might have to do with my bad dreams." No one said anything to Micah as he got up to pace. "Since that thing happened, I've not been sleeping well. I don't know what the dreams are about for the most part, but I wake up, and wake up Reggie too when I scream. She has to hold me for hours afterwards. And then I have to get up. It's getting bad, if you want to know the truth."

"And this is only since you were at the offices where she worked?" Micah nodded at him and leaned against the house as Joey continued. "I've not been sleeping well myself. I don't know what it is that keeps me awake, but I do know that I'm scared out of my mind."

"You two think it has to do with that case and how it was just left open?" Micah shrugged and Joey told Grandda that he had no idea. "Who is this girl? I mean the one that died. What do you know about her other than she may or may not have been involved in the money business?"

"She wasn't involved. Not…she was not human, or not wholly human. Power nearly vibrated off her, but I don't know what she was." He picked up a pencil that had been laying on the band saw and then a sheet of paper. "She had this sigil on her hand. Strange place to have one, I know, but she had one on her right hand that covered most of it."

As he spoke, describing what the sigil looked like and the colors of the sigil, he drew it. The shape of it was nothing Joey had ever seen before, and the more detail Micah put in the drawing, the more Joey realized how hard his big brother had been looking for it. When he was finished, Joey took it and studied it. Taking the pencil from Micah, he made a couple of small adjustments.

"You've seen it?" Joey nodded at Micah, then shook his head. "Then what? Because I have to tell you, this thing is key and I have no idea why."

"It's in my own dreams. Someone...and I have no idea who...but someone has it on them and they're coming after me and another person. I don't know why or where we are, but that thing is the only item that I can remember from my own bad nights. That and some of the creature that wears it." Joey looked out over the expansive yard behind him before continuing. "There's this thing. It's large and it has some human features, but not enough to say that it's like us...and it's powerful. Like magically powerful. And it scares the shit out of me."

"Me too. No creature that I can remember, but there is the feeling that I'm going to be hurt by something that scares me." Grandda sat down on the chair and said nothing as Micah continued with what he'd been experiencing. "I swear to you when I wake up, covered in sweat and my heart feeling like it's about to leave my chest, all I can think about is that if it touches me, whatever it is, I'm as good as dead."

"I can't close my eyes without thinking of this and other stuff." Joey looked at his grandda and brother. "And so you know, I just quit my job. I'm going to turn in my resignation tonight."

He had no idea what to expect. Joey thought for sure that Micah would caution him on not having a steady income. Grandda would go on about how he needed the money for a rainy day. But neither of them did that. Micah grabbed him up and swung him around in a huge circle, and Grandda hugged him over and over, telling him how proud he was of him.

"You should have done it about a month ago." Joey nodded at Micah. "Hey, does this mean I'm fired too? Christ, I hope so. If I have to talk to that dumb woman you have in your office again, I might have to make her a casualty of work. She's about as stupid as anybody I've ever met."

"Paul said he'd take care of her. He thinks that I'm going to take some time off and then come back after I've rested up. I told him I'd give him the resignation tonight by leaving it on his desk, and he told me he'd keep it on file until I was ready. I didn't have the heart to tell him that it was never going to happen. I'll have to call Emmett, of course, but that won't be as bad now that I've done it." Joey felt better than he had in a while. Lighter, as well as full of energy. "I can't believe how well you guys took this. I mean, I have no idea what I expected, but this wasn't even close to it."

"Mom is going to be happy too. She's been really worried about you. She told Reggie the other day that you'd never make it to forty at the rate you're going. Burning the candle at both ends. And Miss May? She was crying the other night when I told her how hard you were sleeping when I left you." Micah patted him on the back and then hugged him again before continuing. "Christ, I'm so glad you did this on your own. I was trying to think of a way to convince you to do it."

Joey talked to them for another hour until Grandda remembered the large trunk he'd brought out. It was filled with carpet samples and wall paper scraps. Mom had sent them to him to help him out after spending the day at the decorators. She told him she'd rather pick out the barn siding than to have to go through that again. Joey laughed at the note she left him telling him he was on his own.

"I guess I should just paint all the walls white, put down brown carpet, and hope that no one notices that all my furniture is from the local salvage place. I have no desire to do this either." They were still laughing when they ordered pizza and beer to be brought out by his brothers. They were going to break in the deck tonight.

~~~

Chris hated to fly. She sat in the seat with her hand gripping the arms so tightly that her fingers hurt. When her dad put his hand over hers, she realized how tense she was when she gave a little scream. He only laughed at her.

"You're going to love this. A private plane is nothing like a commercial one. You'll see as soon as we're up ten thousand feet." Chris groaned. "Trust me, you'll love it."

"I highly doubt that." But even as they made their way to their turn in line to take off, she could feel the difference. First of all, there wasn't a body smashed up against her so tightly that she could hardly breathe, and the carpet under her feet was thick and the seat warm. She glanced at the woman coming toward her with a blanket and pillow.

The blanket was better than the one she had on her bed. The pillow, while small, was nice, firm, and the case on it was silk. Glancing at her dad, she thought of all the things he'd given up to marry her mom, and now he was getting a taste of it again.

Allen had come from money. Not like billions, but his mom and him had been millionaires. His mom had been a great investment banker and had turned the little money that they'd been left when Allen's father had died into a good amount. He'd had his own jet, a nice driver, as well as luxuries that had made it so he'd never had to work a day in his life. Then he'd met and fallen in love with her mom.

Mom had been a hard worker, and Chris and Angel had been everything to her. When they needed something extra for school or for anything else, she'd take on a second, sometimes third job to get it for them. They weren't spoiled, but they were happy. Their father had left them with nothing, less than nothing, as the house that they'd lived in was a rental and their car had been taken the week after he died. Chris had been all of eight when he died, and she and Angel had felt nothing but relief for his passing.

It wasn't like he was mean or cruel to them. But he was incredibly lazy. Sometimes he'd go for months at a time without any job or income. There would be times when he'd be laid off, but mostly it was because he'd gotten fired. He was lazy, pure and simple. His passing had left them with nothing more and nothing less than when he'd been living.

Chris looked down at the mark on her hand. Seldom did she think about what she was, a witch of the highest order that had ever been recorded. A white witch that could do just about anything. But Chris, unlike her sister, had never used her powers much. She would shut a door or maybe bring herself something, but she never used the magic that her mom had passed down to them both. They were both told as children that it was dangerous to use, and would more than likely get them stuck in a lab somewhere being tested like animals. And now that Angel was gone, it was all hers until such time she had her own children.

"Do you suppose he figured out what you are?" Chris covered her hand and put it under her leg. Dad just laughed. "You should know that you can't hide what you are from me, child. I know as well as you do the power that brims around you. You hide what was given to you instead of using it to help yourself, just like your mother did."

"Fat lot of good it did us when we were children. We didn't have a good childhood marked this way." Dad nodded, sadness taking the joy that he'd been feeling away. "I'm sorry. I'm just not sleeping well and I have to deal with this. I think I might just quit my job when I get back and go into my own firm."

She knew that she wouldn't. First of all, there would be no income for a while as she got established, and secondly, it was foolhardy...and Chris wasn't a fool. People did not use a lawyer that they didn't know when the big cases came around. And now with all this other stuff, all the money that they had to pay back, she was going to need to keep her job no matter what. There wasn't any other income now.

"Honey, I'm so sorry for all this. I've tried to reason with the lawyers, but I had no idea when you all moved into that house with me that it wasn't going to be mine forever." Chris waved him off. "My mother wasn't happy with me as a younger man, but I thought for sure she'd changed her mind after meeting you all. She seemed to be so happy when you came around."

Chris had thought so as well. But there was nothing that could be done now. The will clearly stated that once Mrs. Hill died, her son, Allen Hill, would pay back the loan that was given to him in the form of rent that was owed to her over all these years. Also, for the use of the car that barely ran and the money that he'd borrowed from her to help Chris through college; a loan that no one but Dad knew about, and that he'd gone to his mom for when it was apparent that she wanted to be a lawyer.

"We'll figure this out."

She was broke and he knew it. All her money, even her pension, had gone to paying off some of the money and getting them a house to live in. Then Angel had died. Nothing had seemed worth getting worked up over after that.

Chris realized they were in the air when the stewardess came around with a tray of drinks and snacks. Whoever this man was, this Bentley person, he had money to burn. The plane was new, the accommodations were top notch, and the staff was very professional. She would love to see what he did for a living and who his attorney was.

But Chris only wanted to get her sister's information and be done with it. She had only one week to get it and get back before she was into her sick time. And she didn't want to lose that as well as all the vacation time she was using now. But Angel had told her the week before her death that she had something for her, and it would help them with their money situation. Chris had no idea what it could be, or why her sister had felt it was important that she find this man Bentley and get it from him. But she was here now and she'd see to her wishes, whatever they might be.

There was a limo waiting for them when they landed on the small airstrip. The long black sleek thing looked like an animal. She was almost ready to call a cab to take them to the hotel she'd made reservations at, but the man got out of the car and took their luggage before she could run. As soon as their things were stashed away, they were helped into the car by the same man and were off in no time. As they moved through the area, Chris had a moment of panic. Had Dad not taken her hand when he had, she would have begged to be let out so she could breathe.

"It'll be just fine." She nodded at him. "Take a deep breath and just let it out slowly. Angel wanted us here, and when we find out what she had for you, then we'll head back to the house. But I have a feeling things are going to look up for us. I just know it."

"I don't think they could get much worse, do you?" He laughed at her, and Chris settled a little. "If this is how he treats strangers, can you imagine what he does for those that work for him? I mean, this was really nice of him to rent us a car."

"This isn't a rental." She asked him how he knew that. "The driver has a logo on his shirt that says Bentley Corp. on it. And the plane did as well. This Bentley man knows how to live and has no problem spending money when he needs to. I'd bet he's old money."

"I never understood the difference in that. You said your mom was new money and now this guy is old. What does it matter anyway?" He grinned at her. "Okay, I get that he's probably been rich his whole life and that your family only became rich later in life. But what does it matter? Money is money."

"To some. But to this man it will mean very little so long as he has enough to get what he wants when he wants it. I would say that he's worth millions, maybe a little more. He's inherited it from long line of family and they inherited it from their family. It's money that is so entrenched in his life that he doesn't even see it as anything but there."

Chris had always known the value of money, and knew where it was—or in her case now, where it wasn't—all the time. She could not imagine having so much that it didn't matter what things cost or how much you might spend on your bills. It was a scary concept for her.

The gates opened almost as soon as the car paused in front of them. She tried her best not to be excited about seeing the house behind the gates, but she was. So was her dad. He had his face pressed against the window the entire five minute drive up the long driveway. But she knew immediately that he was on the wrong side of the car to see it.

"Oh my goodness." The house, or a part of it, came into view just as they rounded the last of the trees that lined the drive. It was huge, brick, and had a porch around it that begged to be sat on. The large rockers that surrounded the house were white, a startling contrast to the dark brick and blood-red flower pots that sat between them. The long windows were curtain-less, but there were shutters on either side of them. Not the kind that didn't fit the window if you were ever to close them, but real ones that she bet were closed up during storms.

When a man came down the stairs to greet them, Chris had a slight moment of panic. He was huge, and he looked like he lifted houses like the one that he was standing in front of for fun. There was paint on his shirt and jeans, and he looked like he was not very happy with something. As they were helped from the car, the man spoke to the driver and it seemed something wasn't right.

"Hello." She nodded but didn't move forward when he put out his hand. "You're at my house, not my brother's. The driver was told to bring you here, not to…it doesn't matter. You're here now, and while the place is still under construction, we can go in and rest while we try to figure this out."

"Not the right house? I don't understand."

But Chris looked around and she could see it now. The house was being built. There were large dumpsters on the property, as well as several large pieces of equipment. The barn, while it was up and looked ready to receive whatever was going to be stored in it, was only a shell and not complete. She looked back at the man.

"We can just go to the hotel in town." But the man was already unloading their things from the trunk. "Don't do that. We can go now. Tell your brother that we'll meet with him in the morning."

The man stared at her when she tried to take her luggage from his hand. When he moved toward her, his body leaning in a way that made her think of sex and all kinds of things she rarely thought of, Chris licked her lips.

"You should know that I'd like nothing better than to trace your tongue too." Her befuddled mind tried to think what he was talking about when his hot breath blew over her mouth. "Can I kiss you? Just once to see if I'm right?"

"Right about what?" He only chuckled and Chris felt her pussy soak, something that never happened to her. "You're a stranger to me, and all I can think about is letting you...just letting you."

"Then I will." His mouth touched hers and Chris moaned. In the back of her mind, way back, she knew that this was wrong, but as soon as the thought entered her head, she felt it fly away the moment he pulled her body to his. Chris was lost, and she was pretty sure that she didn't care if she was ever found.

Chapter 3

Joey knew the moment that he touched her that she was his…he just wasn't entirely sure what to do with her. But as her body melted against his, her breasts molding against his chest, he had a feeling that no matter what his thoughts were on the subject—any subject for that matter—she was going to be hard to let go once she left here. And he had no doubt that she would leave…Micah was expecting them. Lifting his head, he looked down into her lust filled eyes.

The man clearing his throat behind him reminded him that they weren't alone. Then the slap to his face reminded him that she was clueless as to what she was to him.

Joey didn't want to let her go, but when she lifted her hand to no doubt give him another stinging blow to his face and ego, he caught her hand in his. Her fury only made him want her more, and he knew that the grin on his face wasn't helping him at all.

"I seemed to have forgotten my manners. I should have told you who I was before I kissed you." The man laughed, as did the driver. "I'm Joseph Bentley. You must be—"

"Insane for coming here." She jerked her luggage from him, and he let her have it. She'd have to go Micah's house for a while, at least until he explained a few things to her. "I want to know what the hell you were doing."

"Kissing a very desirable woman." She growled, and Joey laughed. "Do you have any idea how gorgeous you are right now? Christ, I could lay you over this car and take you right now."

The slap was deserved, and he had to fight hard not to laugh when she drew back her fist to hit him. But Joey pulled her to him and around so that her back was to his chest and both her hands were in his. He nuzzled her neck until she calmed.

"I'm going to let you go, but you can't hit me again. I'm not sure that I didn't deserve the first one, and sort of begged you to hit me the second time, but that's enough." She started to struggle again, and Joey rocked into her firm ass. That had her standing still again. "I'm Joey Bentley. My brother is Micah. You must be Chris."

"I am. Let me go." He told her not yet. "I want you to unhand me right this minute. I don't like being treated this way."

"You mean as a very sexy woman?" Joey nipped at her throat and was rewarded with her moan. "Do you have any idea what you're doing to me right now? How much I really want to take you into my house and shove you against the first hard surface and take you? I can't help but wonder if you taste as good as you smell. Do you, Chris? Does your pussy taste like heaven?"

The feeling of heat started at his hands. Then as it grew, Joey knew he was in big trouble. As her magic got stronger, Joey let her go and took a step back. When Chris turned and looked at him, Joey realized that he'd been wrong about her. She wasn't just gorgeous when she was mad, but like this she was indescribably beautiful. Then the power took his breath away.

There wasn't any pain, which at first surprised him. But when he realized that he was still standing, that nothing more than a little discomfort had hit him, Joey braced himself again when she lifted her hands. But she didn't do anything more than stare at him, her eyes wide and her mouth opened. Joey took a step toward her when she swayed, but the other man beat him to her as she fell forward with her eyes closed.

"What did you do?" Joey told him he'd done nothing. "She's never fainted before when she...well, she's never used her magic before, so that might be it, but she's usually so strong."

"What is she? And I know you're more than likely related to her, but you need to hand her to me right now, or my cat is going to be pissed and tear you up." The man didn't move, but he didn't try to fight him when Joey took Chris from him. Joey felt his cat purr along his skin as he held her in his arms. He watched the man, wondering what he had to do with anything that was going on with Micah and his mate.

"A witch. White witch. She and her family have been witches since...well, since forever I guess." He nodded to the car and the driver. "What do we do now? I'm assuming you're something to her."

"My mate." He nodded. "What are you to her? And your name. I didn't get it before, and I think it's important that we establish something before she wakes."

"Daughter. Well, she's my stepdaughter. So was Angel. They were...they were all I had left after their mother died. She didn't use her powers either, my Deb. The only one that did was Angel." The man sobbed a little. "You think that's what got her killed? I'm Allen Black, by the way. And like I said, her stepfather."

They rode in the limo to Micah's house. He was standing on the front porch waiting on them with Reggie and their mom. Joey had told him everything on the way over, and when they got there, the house was ready. Just as Joey was getting out, trying to figure out how to take Chris with him, she woke.

"What happened?" Joey moved the hair out of her eyes and told her he didn't know. "I felt…who the hell are you? And why are you holding me like…like…? You kissed me."

"I did. And you kissed me back." When she struggled to get away from him, he let her. She was scared, and he didn't want to add to that right now. "Are you okay? You nearly took a tumble in my arms back there."

Joey watched the emotions run over her face. It was her eyes mostly that made him think she'd be one to play poker with. They told everything. And when her anger seemed to surge forefront, he leaned back against the seat and waited for it. Joey knew that living with this woman was going to be epic, both in loving and fighting.

"My name is Joseph Bentley. But the only person that calls me that is my mom when she's upset with something I've done. And before you say anything nasty, it's not nearly as often as you think. I'm an attorney with…well, as of yesterday I'm on my own. I have five brothers and —"

"You quit your job? With a firm?" Joey nodded. "Why on earth would you do that? Did you…have you lost your mind? That's good money you're giving up. But I guess you don't need it. That was your house we were at."

"It was and no, I don't really need to work. I enjoy it, but I didn't like working for that firm any longer. I understand that you're an attorney too." She nodded and shifted on her seat. Another tell. "You don't like your job any more than I did mine."

"It's not that. I'm...what does it matter? I have to work and make money. Some of us aren't as rich as Midas." He only grinned at her. "You really think you're charming, don't you? I mean, that good looking smile you have, perfect teeth, and that oh to die for body. But you don't do a thing to me. So stop it."

Joey slid across the seat toward her. "You think I have a nice body? And my teeth are all mine. Would you like for me to bite you to show you?" Snapping his teeth at her made her moan, and Joey pulled her the rest of the way to him.

"Don't do this, Mr. Bentley. I don't have time for a man in my life, and even if I did, you wouldn't be it." She didn't fight him all that hard, and he pulled her onto his lap. When she was seated over him, facing him, Joey pulled her to his cock. "You're not going to make me want you. It's a waste of effort on your part."

"Is it? I think not." He rocked up into her when she put her hands on his chest. "I can smell you. You're wet and hot. I'd like nothing more than to roll you to your back right now and find out just how wet you really are for me."

Her hips began their roll forward, rocking to him with each of his strokes upward. She was riding him hard now, her breaths fanning over his face as she took her pleasure. Joey watched her face, needed to see her when she came...and she was going to, and soon. When she threw back her head, Joey leaned into her neck and bit down on her throat. The taste of her blood nearly had him coming in his pants. Instead, he brought her twice more, pressing his thumb over her clit as she cried out again and again. The last time she came, screaming out his name, Joey pulled her to his own throat and let her smell his scent while he held her.

He was hurting he was so hard. But he did nothing more than hold her. He knew that she was crying and while it tore at his heart, Joey let her. This was just as new to him as it was to her. When she lifted her head from his shoulder, he wiped at her tears and kissed her gently on her mouth.

"This is wrong." He didn't say anything to her but just let her talk. "I'm not...why did we do this? And you can tell me that it was for me, but I know better. You bit me."

"I did. I marked you." She moved off his lap and Joey moaned. His cock was throbbing, and he adjusted himself while she watched him. "I'm not going to take you against your will, Chris. I'm not that kind of man."

"No. But I'm not going to lie to you and say that if you want me, you'd have to take me by force. I want you just as badly as you do me." He nodded, still not touching her. "We can't do this. I'm not sure what you are, but you're not human, are you?"

"Panther." When she looked away from him, Joey pulled her face back to his. "You know what this means, don't you? Why I bit you? Why I had to mark you?"

"You think I'm your mate." He nodded and she pulled away again. "I really don't want this. I know that you've...you've done things to make it happen, but I can't do this right now. Maybe not ever. I've got so much shit going on right now that I can't try and make you understand why this just won't work."

"It will work. It has to." The knock at the window had him realize that his family was waiting on them—on her especially. Joey reached for the door but turned to her.

"You're going to have to trust me on this, Chris. We can and will work out any problems that you have."

"Money can't fix everything." He hadn't mentioned money, but wasn't surprised when she did. He'd investigated her and knew what was going on in their lives. Probably better than they did. "I just need to collect whatever it is that Angel left with your brother and return home. I have a job there that I need to keep."

So many things popped into his head at that moment, things that he needed to tell her. There were people working against them, most of them at her firm. The will with her stepfather's family was another issue that he was aware of, and the problems it was causing them. He only nodded and opened the door.

When she didn't readily take his hand when he offered it to her, he looked into the limo and saw that she was crying again. Joey let her, standing guard until she was finished. When she slid out of the back seat, he took her hand and was surprised when she let him. Joey could have howled at the moon, he was so happy.

~~~

As soon as they entered the big house, Chris asked to use the bathroom. A very beautiful woman with a child in her arms told her to follow her. As they moved down the hall, the woman started talking.

"I'm Reggie Bentley. Micah is my husband. And this little girl is Alexis. Her sister is in the living room with my mother-in-law, Gracie. You'll just love her." Before Chris could ask her why she thought she would, Reggie started talking again. "I've had your things put up in the second bedroom at the top of the stairs. Your dad is across the hall. Milly will be helping you out while you're here, and I think Joey will be staying as well. Here's the bathroom."

Chris looked into the large half bath, then back at the woman. "I don't know who Milly is, but we won't be staying that long for me to need her. And Joey will not be staying with me. I've told him that it's not going to work out. I need to get back to work."

Reggie laughed. "I never said Joey was staying with you. But his house is not finished, so he's going to be staying here, as his trailer has been moved off his property. The furniture that he ordered for his bedroom is late coming." Chris flushed hotly. "And as for it not working out with him, I'm pretty sure that it already has. You smell like him. Strongly too. As for your job...well, when you come to the living room, we'll explain what we've been able to find out."

"My job?" Reggie nodded and the baby in her arms fussed, so she turned to go. "Wait. You can't just say that and walk away. What about my job?"

"The living room is down this hallway and to the right. Second right. The first right will take you to the office. I think Joey is using it right now. Something about a case he's been working on with Micah. So if you need a few minutes with him, then the first right. Anyway, see you down there in a few."

Chris stomped her foot and growled. The laughter that came back at her had her turning to the left. Another beautiful woman stood there with another baby.

"I'm Gracie. This is Anne." Chris nodded and knew immediately that this was Joey's mother. "You're very pretty, aren't you? But you've a smudge of makeup from your tears. I can have Milly bring you your case if you'd like to freshen up a little."

"This house is nuts, you know that, don't you? I mean, everyone around here seems to be on some kind of...I don't know, trip. You're all just too calm and quiet." Gracie laughed. "I'm afraid I'd never fit in here. Even if what Joey said is true, I'm not like you guys. I like it…loud."

"No you don't. You're just used to it that way. Strife and anger seemed to be a big part of your life up until now. Work mostly, I'm thinking. Am I right?" Chris nodded. "We're a big loud family when we want to be. But now, for the moment, things are calm for us. I'm sure a few minutes after going into the living room, you'll wonder why you ever thought we were anything but a loud, argumentative bunch of overbearing, nosey people. But we're family, your family now, and we stick together."

"I don't want that." Gracie patted her on the cheek as she moved by her. "I just want my life back the way it was. I want…I want it to be normal."

Gracie stopped and turned to her. "Oh, honey. Normal is long gone. The bus has not only left the station for you, but has left you no forwarding address and won't return. You're a Bentley now, and you had better get used to us. I'm afraid you're stuck with us."

Chris moved into the bathroom and leaned against the door after Gracie left her. She had a feeling that the woman was right. And Chris thought perhaps she was going to have to keep her guard up in order to keep herself from becoming a part of this group.

Lifting her hands to her face, she felt the mark on her hand move again. Looking at it, she thought of when she'd lifted her hands to push Joey away. Something had scared her to death.

Her sigil looked different. She could see that now. The blue of it was still there, but there were other colors as well. The greens and the reds were new, as well as the yellow that seemed to be wrapping around her wrist and moving up under the sleeve. Lifting her shirt up, she could see that the entire sigil had moved up her arm and was now almost to her elbow. It moved again while she watched.

"No." Pulling the sleeve back down, she tried to think what was happening to her. "No way is this going on. I'm under stress. I'm seeing things."

But she knew better. She was changing with the mark on her hand. The words of her mother came back to her then, just as if she was telling her at that moment.

"There are witches about that can evolve into more. And once they meet their other half, it will make them stronger. There will be nothing that can come between them, and the witch will have power beyond anything that has ever been known to our kind." Angel had asked if it was one of them, but their mom had said no. "We're not that kind of witch. We use ours to make our lives easier. Like when you want a book to read, you bring it to you. You need to know where someone is, you can search. The kind of power that I'm talking about will move mountains, kill your enemies, and destroy your lives. People will hunt you down when they find out. They won't understand it, so they'll try to destroy you and it. Never wish that kind of magic into your lives, my daughters. It is too dangerous for the likes of us."

"How do you know when they have it?" Her mother had touched her fingers to her forehead and she saw it all. The change to their mark, the way their magic grew, and then the way that witches had been burned at the stake. The witch's body had flamed up and then suddenly disappeared in a ball of flames.

"You'd do well to remember that, love. And not let your magic get the better of you, ever. Once people find out what you are, it changes them. Makes them say and do things that will harm you and us." Chris had nodded. "You'll keep us safe, I know that, but Angel will be more…difficult to control. You must keep her close to you at all times. If they find out, people will kill you."

And now it appeared that something was going on with her, and she had no idea what it was. Chris looked at the mark again and realized that it was still growing, still moving. Pulling her sleeve down again, she washed her face and hands and left the bathroom. Without knowing what she had to do specifically, Chris knew that she had to go back home and hide again. There was no way that this was going to change her like it had her mother and sister.

Entering the room that was filled with big men, she nearly turned and left again. But Joey saw her and pulled her into the room. She thought perhaps he'd been waiting for her, but that couldn't be true. No man watched for her. As she was led to the couch, which was near a fireplace that looked large enough to roast several people in, Chris shivered. Joey took her hand and kissed it. Instead of making a scene and pulling away from him, she let her hand settle in his.

"I need my sister's things." Micah looked at her dad, then at her when she spoke. "She contacted me just before she died and said that you have it. If you'd be so kind as to give it to me, we can be on our way and not bother you any longer."

"I was just telling your dad here that I didn't get anything from her. There really wasn't any time." Micah stood up and got a box and handed it to her. "Other than her clothing, this is all that was in the apartment that she was living in. There was food, of course, a few things in her refrigerator, but we went through it all and there was nothing more than that in it. That's all the personal things we could find."

Chris was shocked at how very little there was. A framed picture of Chris and their mom, one of them all at some restaurant years ago, and the wedding picture of her dad and mom. A hair brush, toothbrush and paste, some deodorant, and a bottle of perfume that Chris had gotten her for Christmas some years ago were all that was left.

"She said that she gave it to you." Chris took out each item and looked it over, trying to see if there was a spell on it. Angel had been a great witch. "The last thing she said to me was to find you, that she was dying and that I had to find you. That you had everything. What do you have?"

Tears of frustration made her more upset, but Micah wasn't helping her. None of them were. She wanted to scream, stomp her foot again, and make them understand that she wanted her sister's things. But Micah stood up and grabbed her by the arms, and that was when she saw it.

His eyes told her everything. There she could see the glimmer of her sister, the last minutes of her life. And the way she had given this man, the only man she trusted that was close to her, everything that she had. Everything that made her a witch.

"She did give it to you." He shook his head and Chris nodded. "It's not a physical thing, but her magic. Angel gave it to you."

"How? When?" Chris didn't know but touched his forehead with her fingers and could almost feel the magic, strong and powerful, trying to stay focused within this man. "Is it what has been giving me nightmares?"

"Nightmares?" She moved back from him and he let her. "What kind of nightmares? Do you see who killed her?

The monster that killed her, do you see him in your dreams?"

"I don't see anything. I just wake in a cold sweat and screaming." Chris nodded. While she did feel the magic there, hidden deep within the man, she couldn't see how much there was. But it was powerful. "Can you take this from me? I'd like to be able to sleep at night again."

"I don't know how. I mean, I know that I can get it from you, but I have no idea how to do it. I'm not that strong." She looked away from him, knowing somehow that he could see the lie for what it was. "I know a witch that can help us, but I'd have to convince her to come here. She's not very nice."

"I can handle one witch. Beg her. Tell her I'll pay her what she wants." Chris told him she'd not want money. "What would she want then?"

"I'm not sure. I'm not even sure I can find her. But I'll start tonight." Chris moved away from him and sat on the couch. Joey was there, and when he took her hand this time, she gripped it hard. To contact Myra was going to be hard. To deal with her was going to be even harder. And she'd know what was happening with her too. "I'll try and contact her tonight. Until then, I think we should go to a hotel. It's for the best."

Chapter 4

"What sort of personal problems?" Dick just shrugged and handed him the file. Jackson had been right in the middle of a good game of chess online when his boss just barged into his office saying he had to help out on a case that Chris had been working on. "When is she coming back? I might need a few questions answered if I'm taking this case from her."

"You're not taking it from her, Hill, you're working on it for her while she's gone." Jackson would see about that. "When she comes back, you'll brief her on what you've found, and she'll still be in charge of the case. I just want you to work on it. Or are you too busy fumbling through that game?"

Jackson didn't say anything, but he was pissed. Opening the file, he wasn't surprised when Dick came around to his side of the desk and closed the game. He'd have the guy he'd been playing with all over him when he logged back on, but that was life. Shit happened and he'd just have to get used to it.

"We're not paying you to play games, Hill. You're an attorney for one of the biggest firms in this state. Act like it." Jackson doubted that Dick Roger did much more than he did in a day's time, but he was higher on the chain of command and he could afford to play when he wanted. Jackson was going to be there, someday soon too.

"This is a case about a divorce. I don't do divorce cases." He laid the file on his desk and glared at Dick. "And I'm pretty sure that it can wait until she gets back. What are you really doing in here?"

"You're a lazy fuck, did you know that?" Jackson nodded. "Why my father gave this promotion to you is beyond me. What did you do, have something over him? It must have been good, because my dad doesn't take well to blackmail."

"I used magic." Dick leaned back in the chair and laughed. "You might not want to piss in my oats there, boy, I have a great deal of magic and I'm going to have even more before this is all over. I just have one more thing to take care of and it'll be all mine."

"Whatever." Dick stood up and moved to the door. "Work on the case, Hill, or my dad said he'd find someone that would. And you should know that when you log into your account to play that shit, accounting knows it. Just a heads up."

As soon as Dick was out of his office, Jackson used a little of his power to lock the door behind him. There was too much to do for him to work on a case where two people should never have married in the first place. It actually occurred to him to end one of their lives, or maybe both of them, but he had to conserve his energy. For some reason since he'd come here his power had been draining him. He thought it had to do with Chris.

Jackson couldn't believe it when he'd seen her sigil. It was as if it were meant to be that he not just work in the same place as her but be with her. But soon after working with her on one or two cases, he realized that he'd kill her soon after they started dating, because he just could not stand her. She was a cunt and a power-hungry bitch. And her magic was just lying in wait for someone like him to come along and make it work. For him.

He'd thought about killing her right off. But he was glad now that not only had he waited, but he'd found out more about her too. Her sister. Jackson had done a search on Angel McKenzie and found out that was where the real power was. And she was ripe for the plucking.

But in the end he'd had to kill her…or have someone kill her. She'd been stronger than he'd realized, and now…well, fuck, now all of it was gone. And the creature that had killed her for him was gone too. His magic and body had just disappeared from where she'd been working.

Jackson wanted to know what had happened the day his plan was set to work. And how not only was her body empty of her magic, but Angel had taken out his man, so he had her power. Without either body, Jackson couldn't take it from the monster he'd hired either.

"This is not how I wanted this to work." As he logged back into his account, he bypassed the five messages the man had left for him about stopping a game in the middle, and went to a contact that he'd been using for months now. Since he'd found the family of witches, he'd needed someone to advise him on things that came up. The person at the other end was quick to answer him, which Jackson had found to be very nice. No leaving a message with this person and waiting days for a half-assed reply. He asked the question that was burning him up. What happened to the little shit that was supposed to bring Angel to him whole?

"Have you had any luck finding the croction?"

The croction were a group of beings that worked primarily for witches as hit-men and gofers. Not that they were created for that…that was what he used them for. And no one had complained, so he didn't stop. The one that he'd hired was young and a little high-strung, but he had a good track record with others of their kind.

"Dead."

The single word made the hair on the back of his neck stand up. Few could kill one of them, and if they did manage it, there was hell to be paid for it.

"You are responsible for his death and owe the council for it."

He started typing and then deleted it all. Jackson could point out that he'd only hired the idiot that had gotten himself killed, so it wasn't his problem. That he was dead because he'd not been paying attention, or had bitten off more than he could chew. But he decided he might need something more from the council in the future, and only said that he'd pay.

"Where is the witch, Chris McKenzie?"

The little icon that told him that words were being typed danced along the screen for several minutes. Jackson picked up the file that had been left for him and snapped his fingers over it. Mr. Smith was now dead. His heart attack had just expedited the divorce for the firm. When the words appeared, Jackson read them twice before he finally was able to reply.

"What do you mean, her power is no longer my concern? And I will not cease looking for her. She has something I want and I'm going to take it from her."

The typing began almost as soon as he hit enter.

"Then you go at your own risk. We are no longer here for your questions."

The icon disappeared and the little message box faded out. What the fuck did that mean? he wondered, and tried to log into the account again. There wasn't even a gaming site any longer. Everything, even the icon on his computer, was gone now.

He worked on it for nearly two hours. They had to be there somewhere, and he was going to have some answers. What the hell did they mean, they were no longer there for him? They were the fucking council, a place to answer questions. As he searched for the contact that he'd gotten when he'd first come into his own, someone knocked at his door. Getting up, he nearly snarled at the man standing there when he realized who it was.

"Mr. Roger. I'm sorry, I'm so deep into this case you gave me that I completely forgot everything else. Was there a meeting that I should be at?" The man didn't even bother asking for permission to come in, but nearly knocked him out of the way to do so. "Sir?"

"They're dead." Jackson moved to the other side of the desk and waited. He didn't have time for this, but he knew that this man was his boss. "My grandsons are both dead. Killed just now in an accident when their father was taking them back to my daughter."

"I'm sorry for your loss, sir." Jackson wanted to ask what he wanted him to do about that but didn't. "Is there anything I can do for you? Make some arrangements for you to go to her?"

"No. No. I was...I had just turned it over to you this morning. I wanted my daughter to be happy, so I thought you working on it while Chris was gone would help get it going faster. But then this. Douglas was driving through an intersection, just driving along, when a car came out of nowhere and hit them. The car was...there was nothing left, I was told. Nothing. I'm going down there now. My daughter is going to...I'm going to be there when they tell her." Mr. Roger stood up. "I just came to tell you to stop working on the case. It's taken care of...."

The man broke down. Jackson was never good at emotions, and this was well beyond anything he felt was in his job description. Christ, like he had nothing else to do but hold someone's hand during what they conceived as a crisis. Jackson stood up but didn't move to the man when he waved him away. As Mr. Roger moved out of his office, closing the door behind him, Jackson picked up the file and dropped it in the trash. One less thing he'd have to worry about.

By the time five o'clock rolled around, he was no closer to finding a link or a contact than he'd been that morning. He even tried to get in touch with someone at the meeting place that he'd used when he first came to this town, and they gave him the run around as well. But one thing that was said to him made him keep coming back to it.

"She's out of your reach now. You should just move on." Out of his reach? She was just a white witch whose powers were dormant. It was her sister's that he wanted, and they had been taken from him. Jackson went home and stripped down. It was time to try his own method of finding something out.

The candles were lit by a breath of his air. As he moved into the circle, he started his chant. There was no way that anything could escape him when he sat in the middle of it. As his body began to sway, Jackson reached out for Chris. He was bringing the bitch home, and there would be little she could do against him.

"Come to me."

The wall he hit made his belly jump. Digging deeper within his magic, he tried again. This time he had to lean over and throw up, the pushback was so powerful. Sitting up after dealing with the mess, he tried once again. This time he got something he'd not planned on. The woman standing before him was someone he'd never encountered before. As he tried to wave her away, she laughed.

"Listen up, kid, 'cause I'm only going to tell you this the one time. Leave her be. She's not going to be anything to you now." He told the woman, dressed in red from head to toe, that he didn't want her for anything more than her power. "She's not going to give it to you. Someone else is sharing it with her. You're just shit out of luck, I guess."

"I have powers coming to me from her sister. I want them. I took them and I want them given to me." The woman threw back her head and the laughter bounced around the room and inside his head. Jackson grabbed his skull when it felt as if she was in it, laughing at him.

"You killed her." Jackson said nothing. "Well, you didn't, but you had her killed by one of mine. And that is going to cost you. Or, I should say that it has cost you. Thank you for the payment. Very generous of you. But as for Chris and her sister? You'd be better off trying to fight me for it. You're not going to be able to compete with her any longer."

"With Chris? Don't be ridiculous. She's nothing. Less than nothing. Her powerbase is less than that of a normal human being. I doubt if she could conjure a simple flame, much less take me on. I've grown in my powers, I've been working with them." She only moved around his circle. Jackson frowned when what she was doing occurred to him. "You should have been inside this and I moved out when I summoned you."

"You think you summoned me? Oh dear boy, you don't have that much power no matter how many young witches you kill or work on your own. No, I came here on my own. The witch that you called is...well, she's otherwise occupied." Her laughter rang around him again, this time making his belly sick. "I'm here to tell you...no, that's not quite right...I'm here to warn you.... That's what I'm here for. To warn you. Though I doubt very much that you'll heed it. And to be honest, I'm hoping—"

"Do get on with it." The moment the words left his mouth, he felt the surge of power. Not his own, but hers. As he found himself lifted off the floor, his naked body splayed wide, Jackson felt fear like he'd never felt before. As he struggled to get free, she moved toward him. "I shouldn't have spoken to you that way."

"Nay, you should not have. And I am well within my rights to kill you now, take your puny powers, and end this...this idiotic plan you have thinking you can take the powers of Chris McKenzie." She moved around him and his body, his face, continued to face her. "You're not as good as you think, are you? Oh, you have a few powers, party favors, but nothing more. You can command someone to kill themselves by stepping in front of a bus. And it looks as if you can maybe, after spending a great deal of your power, make a decision in a court room go your way. And I've seen where you used your power to kill a man and his children. Very bad form of you, that one. The man would have been...tolerable; but the children?"

"I don't know what you're talking about." But he did, and he was pretty sure she knew not just that, but everything. She only tisked at him, and Jackson decided that he'd had enough of this groveling. "Tell me what you're doing here. I've things to do and you're not helping me."

"I am not going to either. And so you know, there is no one that will. Not anymore." He asked her why. "I suppose I could tell you. I could let you know just what has transpired since Chris left here. But I'm not going to. This is just too much fun, watching you struggle with trying to get her to bend to your will."

"She will." The witch laughed again. "Who are you? I'm going to report you to the council and have your powers revoked. They will, you know. Only on my word."

Which wasn't even close to being true. He had pissed them off enough to last several life times over these last months, and he'd be hard pressed to get them to—well, answer his questions any more. She seemed to know this too.

"I am Myra." Jackson felt his naked balls tighten to his body; his arms wanted to wrap around him, keep him safe. "I can see you know who I am. And since you do, this warning I'm going to give you will be all you get. Leave Chris McKenzie alone."

Jackson fell to the floor, his circle, perfectly drawn months ago, now a jagged mess over his hard floors. His body felt drained, his muscles like he'd been stretched on a rack. But worst of all was his fear. Myra was not anyone to fuck with, and she'd been there. Warning him about Chris.

Curling into a ball, he lay there, wondering why anyone would care who Chris was or, for that matter, why she was so special. His mind worked through things slowly, but he was exhausted all of a sudden and closed his eyes. Tomorrow he would figure it out, but for now he had to think of ways to get back at Myra and the council that she ran. Things were about to get very hinky, as his brother used to say.

~~~

Chris wandered around the room again. She had no idea how she'd gotten to this room, much less how her desires were ignored. But here she was, in the Bentley house, in a room that was bigger than her new apartment. This wasn't right. When the door opened behind her, she thought about taking a deep breath before speaking, but didn't. Fuck it, this was not her doing.

"What the hell did you say to my dad to make him want to stay here instead of the hotel where I already paid for the room?" Joey just stood there and grinned. "Don't even think about using any charm on me. I'm really pissed off and I want you to know it."

"I do. As does, I'm sure, the rest of the house." She realized then that her voice had been a little high. "May I shut the door and we continue this discussion in a friendlier manner?"

"I'm not in the mood to be friendly with you." He nodded but shut the door behind him and then leaned on it. "What are you doing in this room anyway? I thought it was going to be mine while I stay here."

"It is. Mine is next door. I came to ask you if you wanted something special for dinner. Miss May, my brother's cook, is making dinner now, and she didn't want you to have to eat what we did if you didn't have to." That made sense, she supposed, but she wasn't letting him off the hook yet. "You're a guest here, and Micah and Reggie want you to feel welcome. As for your money for the hotel, it's been refunded to you. He's a friend of ours and didn't have a problem doing that for you. Also, no one will know that you're here unless you tell them."

"Why? I mean, why would it matter if someone were to find out I'm here?" He stood up then and made his way to her. "No touching. When you touch me, I'm not sane."

"I like you a little insane. You're also very sexy when you're furious. Are you still mad at me? You don't seem to be. If not, I was thinking that we could make love before we were called to dinner." She shook her head and backed from him. "No? Why not? You came so nicely earlier, and I'd very much like to see you do that again. With me deep inside of you."

"I don't like sex." That stopped him, and the look he gave her was something she'd seen before. Incredulous. "I've never been any good at it. In fact, that stunt you pulled in the limo was the first time I ever came. Men think I'm boring."

"Boring? How the hell...? Never mind. I don't think I want to know. So the men you've had sex with before...they didn't come either?" She shook her head. "Why the hell not? I mean, I could come just watching you stand there. If you were naked right now, I'd be hard pressed, and I mean really hard pressed, not to simply come without touching you."

"It wasn't their fault. It was mine. I told you, I'm not into it." He moved again, and she backed up until she was pressed against the wall. He didn't stop until he was only inches from her. "Don't do this. I'm not sure why I came with you, but that's not to say it'll happen again. I'm not sexy enough or something, so let's just leave it at that."

"I don't think so." He reached for the buttons on the sweater she had on. "I'm going to prove to you that, first of all, you are extremely sexy. Even dressed this way, all I can think about is what sort of delights you have beneath all these clothes. Then there is the added fact that I can smell you. You're very aroused and I want to drink from you."

"Bite me, you mean?" Joey nodded as he moved his face to her neck again. Tilting her head for him came as natural to her as breathing, and when he nipped at her neck, she moaned, "Why does that make me want to bite you back?"

"I'd like for you to. Bite me until you taste my blood in your mouth. Would that make you come harder, you think?" He was doing all kinds of things to her throat, so when he cupped her bare breast, she whimpered. "Your nipples are so hard. I love their size too. Thick like my thumb. Can I suckle at them, Chris? Can I nurse from them until I get you naked?"

She had no idea if she answered him or not, but his mouth was at her breast and she couldn't have answered him now if her life depended on it. His hands were everywhere, her skin touched, fondled, and then cupped. Her pussy was on fire, his fingers inside of her. Even as she spread her legs for him, giving him whatever he wanted, he continued to bring her closer and closer to the edge. Then he pulled back from her. Chris realized then that he'd stripped her to her bare skin, and she'd not even cared.

"I need you." Nodding, she thought about telling him that she needed him as well. But his shirt was off and nothing could move past the lump that was suddenly in her throat. "My cat does as well. He wants to mark you."

"Mark me?" He nodded and tore his belt from his jeans. She'd never known anyone who wore a belt with a pair of jeans, and watched in stupid fascination while he unsnapped his buttons at his fly one at a time. When he was finished, his hands cupped himself. His cock was so hard she could make out each line of him, the crown of his cock as well as his heavy balls. "Show me."

He pulled his cock free by moving his hands into his jeans and pulling them down an inch at a time. First his crown showed, the thick purple head of it, dripping with his pre cum. Then the vein down the length of him showed. Her mouth watered as he showed her more. When he was free of his pants, his cock stretched from his body like it was reaching for her. And Chris wanted to touch him. Take him into her mouth and suck him as he'd done her nipples.

"Are you ready?" She nodded, not having a clue what he meant, but if he was going to be completely naked for her, then yes, she was ready. As his pants came off, he stood before her, his glorious body hard and bronzed. "Don't run." And then he was gone.

In his place was a cat, a large black one, and Chris nearly screamed. But when he came toward her, sleek and huge, all she could do was stand there and watch him.

KATHI S. BARTON

Chapter 5

Joey watched her carefully. Christ, he wanted to leap at her, take her pussy in his mouth, and have her come down his throat before he marked her. When she didn't run, didn't scream, Joey thought that he might be able to do just that. When he buried his mouth over her pussy, Chris cried out while trying to pull him back.

"Don't. That's not...you're Joey?" He told her he was and licked a path from her knee to her hip before sitting down. "You can talk to me. I mean, you could always talk to me, but like this...you can talk to me."

I bit you. When I took your blood into my body, it made the connection. I can talk to my brothers and other family this way too, but they will never be able to talk to you unless you let them. She asked him if that meant them biting her. *Yes. Micah will need to bite you if you ever become a cat, but for now, it's just the two of us.*

"And you like this, as a cat, you want to have sex with me? I'm not going to like that at all." His cat snarled at him, and Chris backed up closer to the wall. "He's going to hurt me, isn't he?"

No, we're not going to hurt you. Not ever. He licked her leg again, this time brushing over her pussy enough to smell her again. *He wants to drink from you. So do I, but if I let him have his fill of you first, then he'll let me take you for as long as I want. He's a very demanding cat when it comes to his mate.*

"I'm not his mate. I'm not even sure I'm your mate." The cat in him snarled again. "Tell him to stop that. It's scaring me."

He's not trying to scare you, love, but he does want you. As much as I do. But he will let me take you if you're afraid for him to lick your pussy until you come. She stared at him and Joey moved toward her again. *His tongue is longer than mine. Ridged to give you all kinds of pleasure. And the more that he drinks from you, the wetter you'll be for me. I'm going to eat you too, drink you down my throat while you stand there with your legs all spread for us.*

"That's not fair." He noticed that her legs seemed to widen a little, and he told his cat to move slowly. Instead of heeding his words, he moved between her thighs quickly, as if pouncing on her. Then he licked her from gate to clit, his tongue doing just what he'd told her it would. Her legs widened more now, and when the cat in him moved in closer, he nearly begged him to let him take her. But the cat was giving her pleasure, and Joey wanted her to enjoy this.

She came twice before his cat licked her thigh again. When he bit her, his large teeth sinking deep into her flesh, she only whimpered a little before curling her fingers into his thick fur and holding him. He had marked her, as his own mate; his panther had claimed his mate as if she were already a panther. When the cat had his fill, he let him go, and Joey moved to her pussy again. It was his turn.

Chris cried out when he sucked her clit, so hard and firm, into his mouth. Even as he slid his fingers into her sheath, she began riding his mouth. Joey was so close to coming that when she cried out that she was coming again, he drank her down, sipping as much of her into his body as he could catch. Then he stood up. But he couldn't wait any longer. He had to have her. Now.

"I need to take you now."

Her body pressed against his and he took her to the wall. There wasn't going to be any love making this time. He had to fuck her, empty inside of her before he hurt them both. When Joey lifted her up by her ass, she wrapped her legs around him even as he slipped inside of her, her sheath as tight around him as if she had fisted him.

Joey meant to slow himself, pause until he could regain some control over his body. But she moved then, using his hips as leverage to lift her body up and then slam back down over his cock. It was too much and not enough at the same time, and he started pounding her, taking her so hard that he was sure she was going to be sore before he was finished.

"Come for me." Her breath at his throat had him tilting his head for her. "Come, Chris, come for me and bite me. Mark me as your mate."

Her teeth scraped over his flesh twice before he felt her stiffen beneath him. Joey wanted to tell her to come again, but his own climax reared up and took him. As he emptied himself into her, he felt her lick his shoulder, and then her teeth tore at his neck. Joey came again, his entire body tensing up and then letting go as if he were on the edge of a cliff and just fell forward.

Her own scream of release had him taking her again, his body spent but wanting to give her as much pleasure, as much of him as he could. When she went limp in his arms, Joey held her against the wall, almost afraid to move for fear of dropping her.

Adjusting her in his arms so that he held her, Joey made his way to the bed. By the time he laid her down, staggering only once, he smiled as he reached for the coverlet at the foot of the bed to cover her with. Sitting in the chair next to the bed while he watched her, Joey thought of all the things that he was going to have to tell her when she woke. Little of it was going to endear her to him, he thought.

We have company. Micah woke him from a light sleep. Joey sat up, his pants about half way up one leg, the other bare to the floor, and looked around. Chris was still sleeping, so he hurriedly pulled on his pants as he spoke to his brother.

Is it someone I might know, or are you just overly sharing? Micah didn't laugh with him, and Joey felt his cat stir. *What is it?*

She claims she's here for Chris, but she won't come into the house. I'm not sure if she needs to be invited in or she's just one of those people who don't barge into others homes. Joey was coming down the stairs when Micah continued. *I think there is something really odd about her. You need to come and see for yourself.*

There was no one at the front door, so he went to the kitchen. Everyone was in there…Micah, his mom, as well as Grandda and Grandma, Miss May, and Reggie, who looked to be highly amused. But it was the woman on the other side of the door that had his attention. Not so much that she was floating above the ground a good three inches, but she was dressed…well, dressed was sort of an understatement…she was entirely in blue. From her hair that was long and curly to the soles of her shoes. Only her skin, a pale creamy color, wasn't.

"Hello. You're the mate." Joey looked at Micah, who shrugged. The woman spoke again. "This isn't your home. I cannot come inside unless it's the home that you and Chris have."

"It's not complete. I mean, I'm still having it worked on. I've only just started on the barn, and then there is a problem with the.... Who are you?" She smiled at him, and Joey felt warmth. It was the strangest feeling he'd ever had. Like someone had put a nice cozy blanket over him and he was safe.

"The house is finished. I needed it to be, so it is. The furniture is there as well. I set it in the rooms, but you will need to move it where you want." Joey was so confused that he sat down and tried to think. "The young miss, Chris. Is she awake yet? She summoned me, and I'm afraid that I'm running slightly behind."

"Summoned?" Joey stood up now and decided that he was finished with the games. "Did someone put you up to this? Macon? The builder, he said that he was going to find me a magic wand and have the house done for me. Is this his idea of a practical joke? Because I have to tell you, I'm not finding any of this funny."

"I don't do jokes." Joey had a feeling she wasn't kidding about that. "Chris summoned me about some questions that she had. I'm sure she'll have more once you tell her what is going on with her other issues. Oh, before I forget, Jackson Hill is going to be a nuisance as well. I've tried to warn him off, but there is just no telling some people that there is no reason for him to continue."

Joey nodded, then shook his head. He felt like he was on a rollercoaster right now and nothing seemed to be up. When Grandma cleared her throat, everyone looked at her.

Her smile was one that said someone was going to have their butt smacked.

"Perhaps if you would simply explain one thing before moving on to the next, we'll all be able to keep up with you. As it is, you're jumping around like frog legs in a skillet." The woman nodded and moved out onto the deck. Joey looked at Grandma again. "Darling, do go out there and try your best to figure this out. I'm afraid she's given me a headache. I'll go and get Chris for you. Perhaps she can shed some light on this."

"Thanks." He turned to go out on the deck when he thought of something. "Grandma, knock before going in. I think she might be...well, I'm pretty sure that she's...Chris might be...."

He felt his face heat up more and more with each word. He didn't want his grandmother to know what they'd done, even though he was positive that everyone could smell her on him. But he certainly didn't want her walking in on a very naked Chris on the bed. She patted him on the cheek and told him she'd be fine. Joey moved out to the deck where the woman was sitting on one of the many rockers that had only just arrived for his house and Micah had claimed them.

"You'll have some as well." Joey only nodded, feeling stupid again. "Chris is well, I take it? When I last saw her, it was just after her mother passed along. Then there was Angel. She was a good girl as well, but she was a little high-strung for my tastes. But I liked her."

"I'm Joey Bentley. It would help me a great deal if I knew your name. I'm not sure why, but it would, I think." The woman nodded and smiled at him. "You're not going to tell me, are you?"

"Myra. I have no last name. I don't know why I never adopted that custom, but after this long, it seems silly to have one attached to me now. Sit down please, young man, you're making me somewhat nervous." He sat but he wasn't any less nervous himself. "You're going to be fine. I promise. But I must wait on Chris before I can speak freely to you."

He felt Chris then. She was upset, but at what he had no idea. When she was in the kitchen, Joey stood up and turned in the direction she'd be coming from. If she was going to blast him, he'd prefer it was in private. Joey was ready to head her off when she smiled at him. And just like that, Joey fell in love.

~~~

Myra watched the young couple, and what a couple they were. So much in love too. As she listened to their hearts, all she could think about was that she wished she'd been faster in dealing with this. The entire mess was going to take days to fix now. Had she just acted one week earlier, things would have been so much better for them all. When Chris turned to her, she smiled.

"Myra. You certainly know how to make a grand entrance, don't you? And you've upset the household as well." Myra smiled at her. So much like her grandmother it was amazing. "I need to talk to you about some things. And to show you something."

"I've seen it." Chris sat down and Myra was sure had the chair not been there, she might have sat on the floor. "All of it. And this young man too. I can't help that I've upset your household, but I only meant to come here and talk to you. And now that I'm here, what say you that we go to your new home?"

When they got there she still couldn't enter the new house, but they did. It was several minutes before Chris came back to the door, alone this time, and glared at her. Myra wasn't really worried that she'd harm her, but she did want to be on her guard in the event that she tried.

"You did this?" Nodding, she smiled. "What if he hadn't wanted you to do this for him? He might have wanted to wait on the house to be done the conventional way."

"He didn't." Myra laughed when Joey spoke from behind Chris. "I love it. The furniture could use some tweaking, but I love it. I'm sure you will too once you get it the way you want it."

"I'm not living here." Joey just smiled at Chris and nodded, like he knew a great secret and was excited to share it. "I'm not living here. I have a job, and an apartment that I've just signed a lease on. I have a whole other life that doesn't include me living here."

"Darling, perhaps you can invite me in and we'll talk. There is much going on that you need to be aware of, and many things that will...well, let's just say that there are many things that we need to tell you that will have a major effect on your life and that of your stepfather." Chris looked undecided, but she finally nodded. "You have to say it. Invite me in so that I might join you inside."

"I don't know if I want you to be able to come and go as you please." Myra was hurt but said nothing. A lot had happened to her and there was much more. While she could understand the suspicion, it still pained her that Chris didn't trust her. "Come in, please."

The warmth of the house engulfed her. Joey had built this house with love, and he'd planned on sharing it with his mate. He'd not known of Chris at the time he'd started building it, but he'd loved the idea of sharing it with someone someday. As she moved through the house proper to the living room, the things that she'd seen in his mind, the furnishings as well as some of the other things she'd seen there, were perfect for what he'd done.

As they sat in the living room, quiet now as they all had a lot on their minds, Carol contacted her and asked if now would be a good time for her to come. She'd completely forgotten that she'd hired the cook, a witch of some repute to help with not only the everyday things of a grand house, but with the things that were coming to the couple as well. Myra told her to come along and to stay in the kitchen until she called for her. Joey was watching his young bride and Chris was watching her.

"Jackson Hill...did you know he is a witch too?" That wasn't a very nice way to put it, but putting it out there was quick, and right to the point was needed as things were going faster than she'd hoped. "He has it in his head to kill you for your magic. He wanted Angel's, but she'd hidden hers away, hadn't she?"

"Jackson is an asshole. And why the firm hired him is beyond me." Myra only nodded when Chris spoke. When it occurred to her, Myra was as proud of her as she'd been any single person in her life. "He did that. He made himself a partner in the firm. Using magic for one's own gain is wrong."

"He has done a great many things that are wrong." Chris nodded and got up to pace. "He's been warned several times about his use of magic. But the warning has, like most things that he's done, gone in one ear and out the other. He also is responsible for the death of your sister."

"No." Myra nodded. "No. I'm sure he wouldn't have...I don't think he even knew I had one. No one did. I wasn't keeping it from anyone, but Angel told me I'd get full partner if I didn't tell anyone she was a witch."

"And she was right. To a point. But it mattered little what you told anyone. Jackson found out from the registry. He...well, he made himself have access to it some time ago, and that has been troubling us since." Myra waited a few minutes before she spoke again. "He's coming here, love. And when he does it will not go well for him."

"I don't understand. What does he want me for? I have nothing to offer him in the way of power."

Joey cleared his throat, and they both looked at him. The boy was confused, she could see that.

"He killed Angel? For her magic? I guess...what does killing her for magic mean?" He looked at Myra, then at Chris. "And what do you mean, she hid it away?"

"Micah has it." Myra was surprised by that. She knew that Angel was strong, but to hide away her magic in another being was something that few could do. "She must have given it to him before she sent him home."

"Home?" Myra sat up. "You mean your sister parted with her magic into another being, then sent him to his family? While he lived? Oh my, that is very unheard of. That explains...she must have killed the croction."

"Croction?"

While Chris explained to Joey what the creature was, Myra let her mind work. Angel had been a lot stronger than any of them had realized, and it was thought that Chris was the stronger of the two. When she came to her power and that of her sister, Chris was going to be someone to reckon with, and not necessarily in a good way.

Both Joey and Chris stopped talking and Myra turned to see what had startled them.

"Carol?" The woman, a little bit of a thing, nodded. "What is it? I asked you to wait until I called for you. Now I'll have to stop this to explain—"

"There's a...did you know that there is a...? He's here." Joey asked her who. "A vampire. He's here and needing in."

Joey left with Carol, but Myra and Chris stayed in the living room. She wanted to continue with the conversation, but she knew that Joey would need to hear as well. When the large man entered the room with Joey, Myra felt her own magic start to stir up. But he smiled at her. For some reason, that calmed everything about her anger.

"Myra, Chris, I'd like for you to meet my old boss, Emmett Peck. Emmett, this is my mate, Chris, and Myra. I'm still trying to figure out what she might be to us." Emmett stood very still and didn't offer his hand. "Emmett? What is it?"

"She's a witch." Joey nodded but didn't say anything when Emmett spoke again. "I'm not...witches and vamps rarely get along. And if they do, it's not for long. I'm not here to cause any trouble. I wanted to see if I could talk you into coming back to work for me."

"You're safe with me so long as you don't cause me any harm." That was when she noticed that he wasn't staring at her, but at Chris behind her. He was afraid of Chris, not her. "She's very powerful, isn't she?"

"Very." He tore his eyes from Chris to look at her. "You are as well, but in a more...aged sort of way. Experience, I should say."

"You're right both ways." Chris invited Emmett to have a seat and he came into the room. He was watching them both, but he was keeping a close eye on Chris. "I was just telling them about what is going on with their lives now.

And Joey was going to tell Chris about the will of Amanda Black, step-grandmother to Chris."

"Amanda Black?" Emmett looked at Joey, then at Chris as he continued. "Her file came to me about a week ago. There was a problem with it. Richard Roger asked me to have a look at it for him. That's your grandmother?"

"She was." Emmett asked to be excused and when he returned, he had his briefcase with him. "Did my dad ask you to look it over? I'm not sure why Richard would have said anything to a firm that Joey works at."

"He didn't. I mean, I don't think he knew about Joey. But Richard and I were friends. Longtime friends. Anyway, he had this with him one night when we were playing pool. He said there was something off about it, but he just couldn't figure it out. He asked me, with fresh eyes, to have a look at it." Emmett handed her the thick file. "The top copy is the will that was read the week after Ms. Black died. It states the usual things: who gets what, when it should be distributed, and so on. She was a very wealthy woman who, when this was written, had a heart of stone. Then about a month before she died, she changed everything. That will is the second one there."

"Where did you find the second will?" Chris looked at Emmett when he didn't answer her. "You did find it, right? You didn't steal it."

"I had a conversation with her attorney. Just before he died." Myra laughed. She could well imagine what sort of conversation Emmett would have with the man. "He didn't file the new will. He liked the way things were before, the way the estate would be handled. There was some fear that they'd be attorneys for themselves and cut him out of his fees, which there would have been a great amount of, and his firm would hurt from it. So he just let things go the way he wanted them to. I was…I have to file this, but my hands are tied."

"No one made an inquiry about there maybe being another will." Emmett nodded at Joey. "So if no one asked, which why would they, there was no reason for anyone to look for another one. The lawyer was hoping for that."

"Right." Emmett sat down. "So as soon as you or your father inquire about one, we can have this one brought to light. The sooner the better too. The house that you were living in has been sold. I'm sorry about that. But the house that belonged to Ms. Black and all her money is just waiting for the money to come in from the sale of your house so that it can be added to the rest, then distributed. You'll have to work through the system longer if that happens."

Chris sat down, and Myra waited. The girl had one less thing to worry about now. But there was more. Not a lot of things yet, but what there was would ripple down in their lives, that of Joey and Chris, for many years to come. But for now, she let them bask in the joy that their financial worries were taken care of.

Chapter 6

Joey was trying his best not to be overwhelmed by this. He was a levelheaded man. Things like this, magical things, happened. But his house was not only done, but it was furnished, his yard landscaped, and the fencing was up. Even the barn, what had only been a shell of a thing that morning when he'd been by, was now finished as well. A new tractor sat in the middle of it, and there were stalls for the horses that he planned to raise and sell. He turned when the door to the barn opened, and nearly wept when he saw his mom.

"She's talking to your new cook. Chris seems to be as much out of her element as you do. Are you all right?" He shook his head and she laughed. "I can see that. What are you feeling right now, son? Scared, or are you just overwhelmed a little?"

"A little overwhelmed? I'm shooting out of a cannon to the moon kind of overwhelmed. Did you know that Micah has magic in him? Not just his own by way of being a panther, but Angel's. She gave it to him when she was dying." His mom nodded and leaned against the stockroom door. "And then I've been informed that not only do I have a new client list thanks to Emmett, but an office, a secretary, as well as a staff. I didn't know I was going to need a staff."

"I would say that Emmett trusts you or he'd have not wanted this for you. And I knew that you'd grow as you got your feet under you. Not this fast, mind you, but I knew you'd not be able to stay small for long. The magic in Micah? The only people it seems to be bothering is Chris and you. He's fine with it. I'd be more worried about where it goes when it's taken from him." He asked her what she meant. "Her sister left it for Chris. It's hers now. And as her mate, it's yours as well."

"I'm not a witch." His mom only smiled at him. "No, I'm not a witch. So it will go to Chris, not me."

"Joey, look at your arm and tell me what you see." He pulled his sleeve down more. "I see. You were never one to deny things when they were right in your face. What will you do when this man comes calling that wants it?"

"He can kiss my ass." Joey flushed when he realized what he'd said. "I'm sorry. I'm a little tense right now."

"Joey, what do you think your dad would say to you right now? Other than pat you on the back for a job well done. Because as much as it overwhelms you, Myra said that she got the plans for the house and yard from your mind. You did a spectacular job. And Chris will come around." Joey looked into the empty stall as his mom continued. "She's not sure what to think about all this. Can you imagine what must be going through her mind about now?"

"She's terrified. And she's worried that she's in love with me. She told me that. I didn't have the same problem. I'm so in love with her that it aches to think that she might leave me. And Dad would tell me to get in there and make her realize that she loves me, to get on the stick and make the job work, and order those horses we talked about so I can get this dream of ours on the road." He looked at his mom then. "I miss him every day. And now with all this...all I can think about is what he would think. What he would say to me? Then I see you and I realize, he would have told me to talk to you. That you were the smartest person he knew and would have the best advice ever given."

"I loved that man so much." She looked away and Joey felt horrible for upsetting her. When she turned back to him, he pulled her to him and hugged her. His mother was amazing. "Joey, if you don't go in there and make her believe that she loves you as much as you do her and get those horses ordered, I'm going to be very upset with you."

"I've already called Davey. He's excited to be bringing them out next week for me. I've also asked him about a few cows. He said I needed to wait on those. Who knew that cows were more work than horses? I have her ring. Grandma gave me the one she's been saving for me a little while ago." He pulled it from his pocket and showed his mom. "I never saw this one. I guess it was the one that Grandda bought her on their tenth wedding anniversary. But she said she preferred the old one."

"Howie told me once that he wished he'd have gotten her six rings. Once you boys started to come along, she told him that she was going to save this one for you. The one that she wears now will go to Micah." Joey nodded, not really wanting to think of his grandmother passing away to give up the ring. "There are a few other things too. Of hers and mine. She has them all marked for each of you boys, as I do some of the things I have for you. There are some things of your dad's too. Not many...he wasn't one for jewelry for himself. But I did give Micah his badge and gun after he married Reggie."

"He told me." Joey realized what his mom was doing. He was calmer now, his heart wasn't pounding a mile a minute. "I love you, Mom. You've always been there for us, both when Dad was alive and afterwards. You're the rock that holds us all together, and the measuring stick that we try to live our lives by. None of us could have asked for a better role model than you guys. Thank you for everything."

"Good, and I love you. But you need to go into the house now. I think poor Chris has had enough of trying to run things for you." He nodded and started away, but went back to hug her again. After a quick kiss on her forehead, Joey went into the house. His house.

Myra was the only one in the kitchen when he came in. He did noticed that the pantry doors were open, and it seemed to him there was enough food in it for a large army. When he asked her where everyone was, she told him that Emmett had taken Chris to the office and that his brother and his wife were in the living room. The babies had needed a rest. Joey went there first.

"I need a favor from you." Micah told him anything, but Joey noticed that he said it very quietly as Alexis was sleeping. "I need some extra protection around the house until this thing with Jackson is done. And maybe you can help me hire a staff. I think I might have gone a little too big for my first house."

"Carol, your cook, said she had that covered. The staff I mean. I'm not sure what she meant, but I'm staying out of it." He lifted the baby to his shoulder as he stood up and walked toward him. "The extra security is taken care of as well. Emmett has a pack of wolves, both shifter and animal, that is now walking the perimeter. I've also decided to stay out of that. There is too much going on around here to have me stepping on toes. It's all you."

"I don't know how to do this." Micah laughed, startling the baby. Joey reached for her and pulled her little body to his. Just holding her made him feel so much better and calmer. "Well, I don't. When I started the venture, it was to get the house done, then fill it one room at a time. Now it's done. Not only done, but it's really done. And there is a pool in the back that I didn't know about until just a few minutes ago."

"Chris wanted one, Myra said." Joey had figured that, but hadn't found anyone he wanted to ask about it yet. "There are more things you should be aware of. But for now, we have to talk about what this magical removal is going to do."

"Someone talked to you already?" Micah nodded. "See, that's another thing. I'm in the dark about a lot of shit. Not just the security, but everything, including what I wanted to do when my two weeks are up at the firm. Did you know that Emmett purchased a building downtown for me in order for me to stay close to him? He said that...well, it doesn't matter."

"Yes it does." Joey leaned back against the wall, staring now at the little girl as Micah continued. "You're going to do fine with this, Joey. There is a lot going on, but we all know if anyone can handle it, it'll be you. You're organized, anal about a lot of things, but you have to just go with the flow for the time being. There are a lot of people here who are willing and able to help you if you would just let them."

"There's this guy coming here. With the sole purpose of killing Chris for her magic." Micah didn't say anything, and he looked at his big brother. "I can't lose her."

"And you won't. She's a good deal stronger than you think. And I don't even mean the magical part of it. When Myra told us what was going to happen with me giving you guys this magic back, she told her she could do it, no problem." Joey asked him what he meant about giving them the magic back. "You both get it. She's your mate, and I guess you will share it."

Hearing this from Micah, Joey had to accept what his mother had told him, and what he had known deep inside himself. While he wasn't mad about it, he wasn't thrilled either. The mark on his arm was getting bigger, and just an hour ago, he was positive it had moved along his skin just as Emmett came to talk to him.

"Joey?" He looked up, realizing that he was alone and the baby was gone. Chris was looking at him as if she'd been saying his name for some time now.

"I love you." She grinned at him, and he told her to come to him. When she was wrapped in his arms, Joey felt like he could take on the world. "I get so worked up about things. And here you come and make it all right. Will you marry me?"

"Very funny." He lifted her chin up so he could look into her face. While holding her there, he pulled the ring from his pocket and showed it to her. "Joey, what is this?"

"I'm asking you to marry me." He left her to kneel on one knee. She was trying her best to pull him back up, but he took her hand into his and kissed it. The ring slipped onto her first knuckle. "I've been thinking about this for some time. Well, you were never the bride, but I did think about how I would propose to a woman. I think my first practice was to Suzie Lynne. I think we were in first grade. She turned me down flat and then kicked me, if I remember correctly. Then I just practiced in the mirror."

"You're insane." He might have been, but he felt smarter for asking her to be his wife. "Get up before I take you seriously."

"I wish you would. I love you. I don't think I say that to you enough. But I do. With all my being. And I want you to be my wife, for all of our lives together. Have children with you, go on vacations together." Joey pushed the ring up more on her finger until it was flush with her hand. Then he looked up at her. "I'm a good man. Not as good as some, but I'm not too bad. I leave my socks in weird places when I'm in a hurry. I never eat a good breakfast. Too much on my mind. And I rarely know what the date is. I might know the month, but that would be stretching it. Will you please marry me, Chris?"

Instead of answering him, she got down on her knees to face him. He was slightly nervous when she reached into her own pocket and pulled out a ring that he'd seen every day of his entire life. This woman would never do things in the norm. She kissed his finger as he'd done for her.

"I was going to get you a ring. Seriously I was. Then all this happened and there was…never mind. Your grandda saved the day. He said that none of his grandsons are ever prepared, and he thought perhaps it was his turn to lend a helping hand. But I have to give this back to him when I get you one. Okay?" Joey nodded, thinking how when he told her yes, he was going to find his grandda and hug him until he couldn't breathe. "Joseph Bentley, I am an honest person, so I'm going to tell you that you're insane for wanting to marry me…but will you? I can't believe that we're even talking about this after just two days. I'm a slob when I'm working. I have no socks because when I wash them, one always comes up missing, so I just quit feeding the dryer. I don't eat right, but I have a feeling that with a cook, that might change. I love you. I should have said that first, but I do. I never thought I'd even like you, but I love you, so go figure. What else? Oh yeah. I want to be your partner in your firm, please. I'm a good attorney, and have only lost one case so far. And I want to live here, in this too big house, and fill it with babies. Will they be babies?"

"Yes." She asked him what he meant. "Yes to everything. Yes, I love you too. Yes, I want you to be my partner. Yes, let's fill the house with babies and yes, I will marry you."

"Good. There's just one more thing." He nodded, not caring one whit about what else went on in the world around him. "There's a man outside that says he has some horses for you. But if you let him take the other ones to the slaughter house, I'm never going to forgive you."

Joey stood up after Chris slipped the ring on his finger. Grandda would have to wait. Taking Chris's hand, he made his way to the yard to find his entire family there with Davey and two trailers of horses.

~~~

Chris watched as Joey talked to his friend. The trailer that had the horses that were staying was already unloaded, but the other one was sitting there unattended. When Tony came up to her, she looked at him and he winked.

"You want them?" She nodded. "Then you have to take full blame for what we're about to do."

"Okay. What are we about to do, and how much prison time are we talking?" He only laughed at her as he moved to the back of the trailer. "You're going to just let them go?"

"No. Grandda is over there with Micah. They're going to try and get them in the other fence. And Myra said she'd make sure that they went there. I didn't ask her how."

Probably a good thing, she told him. "Okay. I'm going to do the heavy part and you're going to take the blame by just opening the doors. But stand back. Davey said that they're hurt and one of them is a little off."

The handle was lifted without a sound. She wondered if he'd done something to make it that way, as the one with the six horses in it that they had put in the barn had sounded like a woman was being murdered. But as soon as the doors opened, she looked into the trailer and her heart twisted.

"Oh baby." The first two horses ran out of the back end like they'd been set free from prison. The last one looked at her with the most incredibly terrified look she'd ever seen. She moved into the back with him just as Tony cautioned her to be careful. But her entire focus was on the horse.

He'd been beaten. Not recently, but not long ago either. She moved her hand over his nose and he shied away from her. After the third try, she realized that not only had he been hurt, but was probably blind too.

Taking the long rope that had tied him, she led him out of the trailer. As soon as the sun touched him, he jerked away from her but she held him firmly, talking to him as quietly as she could. He came with her, but she knew what it was costing him. Leading him over to the open gate, she walked in with him instead of just letting him go. Chris heard the gate close behind them.

"Chris, come away from him." She looked at Joey and Davey when Joey spoke again. "Honey, come here. He's dangerous. Davey said that he's killed and he is mean. Something is wrong with him."

"There is. He's hurt, the poor thing." Remembering that she had part of a pear in her pocket, she pulled it out and let him smell it. She held it in her palm as she continued to talk to him and Joey. "The poor thing can't see, did you know that? Someone beat him so badly that he's blind now. Who would do such a thing? They need to be beaten too."

As he slowly ate the pear, she talked to him. When it was gone, even the core, she was pushed back when he touched his head to hers. She had no idea what he was doing until Davey told her what to do.

"He's greeting you, Mrs. Bentley. Bump him back." Chris told him to call her by her first name and did what he told her to do. The horse put his head over her shoulder, and she hugged him to her. "Well, I'll be damned. He's hugging you. Christ almighty, he's hugging you."

When he left her standing there, she looked at Joey. "I would like to keep him. And the other two. I don't want them to go to the slaughter house. I think...I can help them." Joey nodded and she moved out of the gate. The big horse followed her. When she turned to him again, he bumped his head to hers before moving away. She supposed he could smell her.

Joey hugged her to him and told Davey he'd take them. "And if you could also swing the other, I'd be very grateful to you." Chris asked him what that was. "We've just hired two hands to help us with the ranch. Congratulations, Mrs. Bentley, we're attorney ranchers."

A vet was called out to look them over. Chris moved up and down the fence line and Elwood—the horse's name— followed. A bag of apples was brought out for her to give the others too, but he never left her. When the vet finally arrived, he took one look at the horse, then at her.

"You do know that he's set to be put down. The previous owner said he killed one of his best mares, as well as injured one of his hands." Chris nodded and asked him if the man had beaten him. "Not that I'm aware of; but then,

I've only seen pictures of him. The horse, not the man. They said he was too wild and too mean to handle."

"No he's not. I've been with him, and the most he's done to me is hug me. Oh, and steal part of my lunch." The vet, Heath Berger, nodded and made his way to the gate. Before he got within a yard of Elwood, the horse started to scream. Chris moved to hold him, wondering if it was the smell or something else.

"Now see here. You want him to tell others what a bad pony you are?" He nodded. "No you don't. You're a good boy and I'm going to make sure no one touches you again in pain. I'm a good attorney and I'll represent you. All right?"

When he nodded again, she turned to Heath and told him to come on. Elwood stood still, but she could tell he was afraid. His eyes kept darting to the man, then back at her even though he couldn't see them, but she was sure his sense of smell was as good as Joey's. Chris kept talking to him during the entire exam. When he was finished, the vet just shook his head.

"The poor thing has been abused for some time, if the scarring is any indication. Some of these are a few months old, others years old. It looks like someone has taken a whip to him recently too." Chris asked him about his sight. "He's blind. Not sure what might have done that, but I'd say he might have had an infection and no one cared for it. You really going to represent this horse?"

"I am. No one should be allowed to abuse anyone, but animals have no one to protect them." Chris asked him if he'd write her up something that talked about the abuse. "I need to document this for him."

"I'll do you one better. I'll make it my business to make sure that the rest of the horses on the farm aren't treated like this. It's well within my ability as the county vet." Chris thanked him. "No, ma'am, thank you. Someone…me included…should have gone out there and checked on him. And the other animals he has out there."

Joey came to stand beside her and nodded to Heath before speaking. "I have to talk it over with my wife here, but I've just had a long conversation with Davey. He said that you know of a couple of other horses that need a second chance. I'd like to help them out. Bring them here to see if…I don't know, I guess see if we can help them out too. I understand that you're looking for a place to hang your hat after you retire."

"I am. And I will." Joey asked him what he meant. "I would love to be your vet for this. The missus here just told me that she's going to represent these animals, and I'm going to help her too. You're a good man, Joey. I heard it, but now I believe it."

After he walked away, telling them that he'd be back in the morning to see if he could save one of Elwood's eyes, Chris turned to Joey. He was red in the face from something, and she decided to have a little fun with him.

"Okay, Missus? No. I'm Chris, or the wife, but never the missus of anything." He nodded. "And if you think you're going to have this grand idea and I'm going to nix it, then you're dumber than the man who hurt this guy. And let me tell you, he's going to pay out the ass for what he did to my new friend. Another thing, I—"

"I love you too." She nodded when he kissed her. "Now. My family is staying for dinner, and then you and I are going to go to our room and I'm going to fuck you until you can't stand up. Then for scaring the shit out of me for going into the trailer without help, I'm going to beat your ass before I make love to you again."

86

"I love the way your mind works. And you should know that I had help. He said I'd have to take the fall, but I'd really like to find a way to help your brother out. I think...what happened to Tony?" Joey looked at the brother in question, then back at her. "Are you going to tell me, or do I have to wait for him to tell me?"

"I think him. He's been...hurt does not even begin to cover what was done to him." She nodded and glanced at Tony when he yelled for them to come and eat. "It's not physical, honey, but it was bad for a long while. I don't know if he'll ever get over it."

"He will." Joey wrapped his arm around her, and they went to the house. "Oh, and I have a job for you and Burke later. You're going to help me with the horse asshole, and Burke is going to make sure that he doesn't die before I'm done with him."

"Deal. And just for fun, I think we should take all of my brothers. They might be able to...assist you in this too." She nodded as they entered the house.

Chris looked around the table, their new table, as they all were seated. The babies were even in the room in a small crib that had been brought in by Myra. This was family. Her family, and she was thrilled to death to have become a part of it.

To think that not three days ago she was scared to death to come here, and now she couldn't imagine leaving. It was the strangest, most wonderful thing that had ever happened for her.

Chapter 7

Jackson checked into the hotel just after five-thirty in the evening. He had had to work hard to get this information from Dick, but in the end he'd seen that what he wanted was a good enough reason for him to have it. What he told Dick was that the case he was working on needed Chris's touch, and that had gotten him the address.

"I'd like a wake-up call at ten tomorrow morning." The man who had carried up his bags said that he would let the desk know for him. As his luggage — one with clothing in it, the other some of the items he might need to bring Chris to his way of thinking — was all he'd brought, tipping the young man fifty dollars would get him the rest.

The shop that he was looking for was within walking distance of the hotel. It wasn't the grand kind of magic shop that he had at home, but it would do. According to their website, they catered to all sorts of spells and magic. Jackson was excited to go and see just what kind of things they had.

After seeing to his things, he decided that he'd get some dinner and check it out. As he made his way to the little shop, then on to the diner that the front desk recommended, he thought about what he was going to say to Chris in the morning. They would talk a little. He had a list all set up. Then he would show her what he was. A grand witch. Jackson knew that he wasn't one yet…a grand witch…but he would be soon. As soon as he had Angel's power and added it to his own, he'd be something close to it. And then he'd have enough juice to work on building himself up to the next level until he was on the grand scale. And that was where the magic was.

He hated being a lawyer. It hadn't been that hard to get into college or to get through it. Especially the way that he'd made his way through. Magic had not just made him what he was today, but had also gotten him the good grades that were required to work for the firms that paid well. And ultimately, that was all he cared about. Money.

It funded his needs. A way for him to purchase what he wanted when he needed it. It had also opened a great many doors for him. Now it was as if information on witches and what kind of power they had simply fell into his lap. He might not have gotten this far had he not had a list of them practically handed to him on his first case.

The woman had come into his office one day, and there had been a recommendation from one of the partners that he take the case. The first thing out of her mouth had been that she was a witch, and if he had a problem with that, he should tell her now. When Jackson had looked up at the doorway to the room he was using, several of the other personnel, as well as the partner that had told him about the case, were standing there laughing. It had been a joke on their part, but they had no idea that he was going to make this work. Even if it was only in his favor.

She'd been harassed at work, she told him. The boss had told the others that worked with her what she was, and they had been relentless in their jokes at her expense. Someone had painted her car black, then put a large dead cat on the hood. Another time a group of them had gone to her home when she'd been working and had painted the words *witch cunt* on her doors, and had put a mannequin on the front lawn burning at the stake.

"Like they did in Salem a long time ago. Why the hell would they do something like that? Was it supposed to, I don't know, scare me off what I love?" Jackson had asked her what her level was. "Three. I'm a three. What are you?"

Jackson had told her he was a three as well, when in actuality he'd only been a one. A first-year witch. But he was working on more experience than she was. He'd been at it for a lot longer than he'd been in a coven. So as they continued to talk about their love of magic, she'd given him a list of places he could go to get some extras. Some of the things that they didn't sell in the local stores.

She'd lost her case, of course, but they had dated for about a month. Not that he would normally have dated someone like her. The woman was beneath him in so many levels that it wasn't funny. While she was content to stay where she was in the magical world, he wanted bigger and more. But there was information that was worth more than any kind of relationship she might have thought they were having. The woman believed him to be her soul mate right up until the time he plunged the dagger, one she had suggested that he buy, right into her beating heart. It was his first of many such murders for his cause.

The shop was bigger than it looked from the outside. He knew when he walked in that this place was going to serve him well over the coming days. They had things that he'd only just read about; herbs that were drying above the shelves alone were enough to make him salivate with greed. And when the owner of the place came out to help him, Jackson fell in love. Not with her, but the shop and its contents.

"We been here for nine generations now. Most of the things we carry, we make them ourselves. I have a drying room on my property that I use almost every day to dry this and that." He nodded, making a mental note to fill the back of his car before leaving this dump of a town. "My great grandmother is the one that did the magic on the size of this place. She had to when we started to grow well beyond the doors and walls. We'd be out of business if I had to pay rent on a place that was even half this size. But she put a little of her own magic into it, and now we have more room than we can use sometimes."

"I didn't think this place was this big when I was outside. She did an excellent job. I would have thought others would have noticed it by now and remarked." Paula shook her head and told him it didn't work that way. "I'm sorry. I don't understand."

"The ones that have the touch can see what she's done. Others, humans I call them, they can only see what they want to see. A pickled kidney of a frog in a jar they see as some black candles that are marked magical. We both know that none of that is useful, now don't we? We have spells that call for stuff that I carry, but the humans, all they see is the things they see in the movies." She laughed when an older couple came in with their cameras out. "See what I mean? They're waiting to see someone come in on a broom so they can go home and tell their friends what they seen. The girls that work for me? They'll dress up on the weekends, when we're the busiest, and let them have a show, but we're just witches trying to make a living."

Jackson ended up spending nearly five grand in the place, with plans to spend more when he got home. She was shipping it all to his house, and it would be waiting for him when he got there. But he did take a few things with him. Some of the items that he did need to take care of Angel and her magic.

His walk to the diner was made with a lighter step. His little black bag was not marked in any way, but he was excited about it. The place, *Mamma's Home Cookin'*, was brand new, he'd been told, but had actually been there for many years before it had burned to the ground some months ago.

The menu was simple…almost too simple, he thought. There was breakfast on it that had pancakes, eggs, or waffles. And with that you could get bacon, sausage in links or patties, as well as ham. Then there was toast or biscuits and juice. Then, of course, coffee or tea. Lunch was either a burger with or without cheese, a grilled cheese sandwich, or you could get a ham sandwich. A list of cheeses were beside each choice. There were fries that were not baked, whatever that meant, or chips. A list of sodas and the coffee and tea. Dinner was just called dinner.

The waitress told him his choices. "We have meatloaf with mashed potatoes, gravy, and green beans, or you can have either a pot roast dinner with the same sides or fried chicken. You get a house salad with that and some bread. The chicken takes about twenty minutes, 'cause we fry it up to order."

Jackson had no idea what that meant but said nothing. He wasn't really in a hurry, so he ordered the chicken. She told him again that it was going to be a while. After assuring her that he was fine with that, she brought him back a basket of rolls and a bowl of butter.

Not one to partake in bread all that often, he pulled out one of the large rolls and was surprised to find it hot and so soft it nearly fell apart in his fingers. Pulling it apart to eat only half of it, he found himself smearing the creamy butter all over it and devouring it before he could even worry about the calories. The second, then the third roll was gone before she brought him his iced tea. With a grin, she told him she'd give him some more.

The salad was better than he'd thought too. While he'd expected just lettuce with the usual carrots and cucumbers in it, he found himself nearly licking the bowl clean when he discovered that it also had a healthy offering of real bacon bits, sliced eggs, as well as homemade croutons. By the time his dinner was brought to him, Jackson had finished off two more baskets of rolls, much to his shame, as well as a second salad that he was informed was going to cost him another dollar. Jackson would have gladly paid her ten dollars for another taste of the dressing alone. When he asked her what it was, all she told him was house. He supposed he'd have to leave it at that. But he was going to try and get a bottle of it before he left. Jackson knew people that would figure it out.

The dinner was set before him, and all he could do was stare at it. Not only was there a mound of the whitest mashed potatoes he'd ever seen, but the creamiest gravy had been poured over it. The green beans were plentiful too, and as soon as he put the first bite of them in his mouth, he also knew that they had not come from a can. Someone had taken the time to snap fresh ones. But it was the chicken that had him moaning out loud. And there were four huge pieces of it.

94

There was a crust on it. Not like a pie crust, but a thick breading that had him thinking of his grandmother and her scald, as she called the breading on her own recipe. He cut into what he thought was a breast and watched the steam pour from the cut; the juices of the chicken seemed to bubble up right before his eyes. And when he took his first bite of the succulent meat, he closed his eyes and hummed his pleasure. Nothing this good had ever crossed his lips before.

When the waitress came back to refill his roll basket, he asked her how long the cook had been at this. She smiled at him, and he knew that he was just going to love the answer.

"Up until about a month ago he was living in a box behind the mall. Miss Reggie snatched him right off the street and cleaned him up. He was so grateful for her help that he shared his momma's recipes, and she said to him if he brought in customers she'd sign the building over to him in one year. I think he's gonna make it, don't you?"

Jackson looked around. That was when he noticed that every table was filled, not with just one or two people but with groups of them, sharing a table with strangers so they could eat here, she told him. There was a line too, not around the block because of how large the dining area was, but out the door and into the street. There were to-go orders being handed over the counter too, as well as money hand over fist. Whoever owned this restaurant was making more money than he was as a lawyer, he'd bet the house on it.

Jackson decided that he was going to be here for every meal while in town, and he was going to have to find the owner. The idiot could not just give this place away to a homeless man. He would take it off his hands in a heartbeat. This would be a place he would make enough

95

money to have fun in, and the little hope down the street would supple him with the means to do so.

As he made his way back to his hotel, almost too full to move, his phone started to ring. Pulling it out, he nearly laughed when he saw who the caller was. Chris couldn't have had better timing. He answered it like he felt. Full of great food and cheer.

~~~

"I'm not your darling, Jackson. I've asked you to not call me that numerous times. Now it's bordering on being harassment. What are you doing here in my town anyway?"

"Your town? I had no idea that you were so rich that you could afford your own town. But that's neither here nor there. I'm here on business. I've come to talk to you about the Benton case. You do remember that case, don't you? You left it on your desk when you left town so quickly." When he paused, she looked down at her notes. Everyone in town had let her know that he was there, and she was going to figure out why. "Could it be that you've found yourself a boyfriend and he's taking up a lot of your time?"

Joey nodded for her to go with it. "As a matter of fact I have. We're getting married in a few days."

Silence. Chris looked at Garth, who was helping them with the questions to ask. Some of them were really strange, but she said she'd stick with them. When Jackson laughed, she thought perhaps something else was going on, but then he spoke.

"You nearly had me there, Chris. I can't imagine anyone that would get married only after a few days. You're much too smart to let someone take you for a ride." She asked him what he meant. "Oh, I don't know. Or are you marrying this man so quickly because he has money? Does he know how much you owe the estate of Mrs. Black? I'm sure that he'd run for the hills should he find out about that. Perhaps I'll let him know. Or I won't. What will you give me if I don't tell him?"

"He knows how much I got from the estate, but that matters little to him. He's richer than my family was." Jackson laughed again. "Were you just trying to blackmail me, Jackson? Not very smart of you, if you ask me."

"You can't have any money, Chris. You forget that I work in the same building you do. I know what the old bat did to you and your dad. Took him for a ride too, didn't she? And the firm knows now too. I made sure that they knew that you and Black are related. Imagine their surprise when they found out. But you never answered me about what you're going to give me. I have more dirt on you than you can imagine." She was getting mad, but Garth and Joey told her it was fine. "Like how your sister was a witch. As are you. Not much of one I've heard, but still, not a good image for the big firm."

"I quit there this morning." Again he was quiet, and that was when Joey pointed to the next item on the list. "Myra sends her regards, by the way. She said that you've been ousted by the council. That must have hurt. And Angel was a powerful witch. I have her magic."

"What do you mean you have it? It should be mine." When he said that, Garth pointed to the next question, but Jackson spoke before she could say anything. "You'll be giving it to me as soon as I see you. I've plans for that. And as for the council, I'm not worried about them. Soon enough I'll be in charge of it, and things will change then."

"Did you kill her?" Jackson laughed and told her that he'd had her killed. "Why? What did she ever do to you?"

"Nothing, but for the fact that she had something I wanted. And now you do. What do you suppose is going to happen to you now?" She didn't answer him because the pain in her heart was twisting her up inside. "Nothing to say, Chris? I knew what you were the week before I came to work at the firm. It was my plan to kill you for your little bit of magic, but then I found out about your sister. And there was some power. But it was lost to me."

"You're confessing to murdering my sister and that you plan to kill me too?" She looked at Joey when he touched his fingers to her cheek. "You killed an innocent woman just for her magic. What kind of sick bastard are you?"

"A smart one. And I don't know a great deal about the law, because let's face it, we both know that I didn't crack a book while in college. But I do know that you can't use what I say to you because you'd have to be able to prove it. And I don't think you can. Unless.... You aren't recording this, are you, Chris?"

She was but said nothing. Garth pointed to the next question. "You lied about your boards too, didn't you? When you got your job with Roger, Roger, and Rocklin?"

"Of course I did. I had to be close to you." She looked at Joey, then at the man sitting across from them. When he nodded and stood up, Garth moved away too. He was at his computer in seconds, clicking away at something, when Jackson spoke again. "I'm coming to find you, Chris. And when I do, I want you to be ready to turn over everything. I'm not fucking around with you any longer. I've found that...well, this town might be too small for the two of us. So I'm afraid you're going to have to go. One way or another."

"You mean you like my little store on Tenth, the House of Magic? I had to figure out a name quickly, and was afraid that it would just be too simple. But apparently you're just a simple kind of man. You saw just what I wanted you to see. But I have to be honest. If you look in your little bag, all you're going to find is papers that are nasty with dirt and mud on them." She laughed then. "How about the chicken you had for dinner? Did that fill your belly? You should have taken a better look at what you were eating, Jackson. You might have seen what was really on your plate. Were the maggots as tasty as I made you think they were? And the rolls. Mary said you had five baskets of them. She did tell me that she wrapped up some for you to take with you. Maybe you should have a little peek at what you've been eating."

Waiting, she knew just when he opened the large container. The chicken that he'd left on his plate had been put in the box, as well as four more rolls. When he started retching, loud belly emptying noises that made her own jump in protest, she heard someone ask him if he was all right.

"No, I'm not fucking all right. Look what she had me eat." The person, whoever he was, told him he was sick. And Chris had a feeling that he was going to be a good deal sicker before she was finished with him. "You fucking cunt. You're going to pay for this. Who feeds a man rotten meat? And what is that putrid smell coming from that bread?"

"Feces. I had it brought in from the nearby dog pound just for you." He was puking again, and she laughed. It was nasty and cruel, but no one deserved it more than Jackson did. When the line went dead, she figured that he'd either hung up on her or he'd dropped the phone. Chris looked at the people in the big room that was going to serve as her office when she started working with Joey.

"Remind me never to piss you off." Chris nodded. "Nor to allow you to cook for me when you are. You're a vicious person when you want to be, aren't you?"

"I never knew I was until this." She stretched out her legs, putting them across his lap. His cock started to thicken as she moved her feet over him. "You're going to find it difficult to walk if you keep that up."

"I don't plan on walking all that far. You're going to use a little of that awesome power of yours and make everyone go away. Then you're going to let me lay you across this table and feast on you." Chris wondered if she could do it when Joey pulled her shoe off and started to roll her foot in his strong hands. "What I'd really like to do is have you suck my cock. Then, when you've made me come, I'd watch you while you brought yourself to peak."

The agent from the FBI left them first. If she knew his name, she didn't remember it now. Then she told Garth to leave them. He stood up, looking slightly confused before he left the building too. The last two men, workers who were trying to get their new offices up and running, just closed up the paint they were using and walked out. Chris locked the door when they were alone.

"I had no idea I could do that." Joey nodded and stood up. He was undoing his pants as she dropped to her knees in front of him. "I'm going to have to have some sort of incentive to make you come. What if I don't want to play with myself to come? Maybe I'd like for your panther to eat me."

She saw him then, the great black panther, as he moved over his skin. When she put her hands up on his chest under his shirt, the feeling of his cat seemed to be all over her. Freeing his cock, Chris took him into her mouth and swallowed him. His cry of pleasure had her looking up at him.

"I'm going to come if you do that again." Chris nodded and swallowed him again. He didn't come, but she could taste him. His own thick cream was filling her mouth as she rolled her tongue around him when she lifted her head.

As he fucked her mouth, gently at first then harder, she unbuttoned her blouse and freed her breast. Tugging at her nipples, she could feel her pussy swell with need, and she knew that she was wet. Sliding her fingers up under her skirt, she touched her clit and moaned around his cock.

Before she could do it again, bring herself to climax, she found herself on the desk, her panties gone and Joey's panther between her legs.

"Eat me."

His head lowered to her even as she cried out her first release.

Chapter 8

Joey wanted to fuck her, eat her, and then come all over her all at once. But his cat had wanted her too, and he knew that she loved it. When she screamed out her release before he'd even touched her, Joey encouraged his cat to enjoy her. And he did. Over and over.

As soon as his cat was ready to let him have his fill of her, Joey took his body back and slammed deep into her. Holding her still while the table moved across the room, all he could think about was that she was his. Now and forever. Taking her breast into his mouth, he bit down on her nipple before sucking hard on just the tip. The taste of blood filled his mouth even as his balls tightened to his body. When she came this time, her fingers tearing into his back, Joey let his cat go enough to mark her again while he filled her with his cum. Christ, he ached when his balls filled a second time and emptied deep within her. Joey threw back his head and pounded her until he couldn't move. Dropping atop her, he only had one thought. She was both their mates.

Her fingers jerking his head up from her had him snarling loudly. Joey thought for sure he'd hurt her when he saw the tears in her eyes, but she told him she was happy. Happier than she'd ever been.

"Turn me." He was dazed for several seconds before he asked her to repeat herself. "I want to be like you. A panther. Do it. Change me. I want to taste you like you do me."

"It's painful. I don't want to hurt you." She told him she didn't care, that she wanted this now. Joey felt his cat snarl at him. He was telling him that she was theirs, in all ways, and that he should do it. Joey felt his teeth shift in his mouth, like they did when he shifted. When Chris told him again to do it, Joey let his cat take him and he tore into her soft belly.

Her scream had him thinking that he'd killed her. But her hand curled into his fur and she told him she was fine. To not stop. Joey looked up at her through his cats eyes and could see the pain she was in.

I should have waited. Her small laugh had him aching more for what he'd done. *You might die. I don't even know what I was thinking. Micah is going to kill me.*

"I'll eat him alive if he touches you." She was weaker now, and he told her to stop talking. "I wanted to tell you that I love you. And I think I want to have children right away with you. Do you think it will hurt Reggie if we do?"

It took him a few seconds to realize what she was talking about. *No. She has her daughters now, and I think she's as happy if she'd given birth to them herself. Honey, please let me stop this. I can have Burke or Nolan here in a minute.*

"You stop this now and I'll never forgive you. Where do you have to bite me now?" He realized then that she'd planned this. Had talked to someone to see how it was done. "Joey? Where? I can't think right now."

Your thigh. I have to bite you hard enough that it breaks bones. She told him to do it. *I can't, love. I've hurt you enough.* The slap to his nose had him backing away from her.

"You want Jackson to be able to kill me? You want him to win? And I so am looking forward to running in the woods with you. And licking your cock until you come." She lay back down. "Do it, or so help me I'll call Micah in here and tell him you're a pussy."

His cat whimpered but moved to her leg. When she lifted it up, his cat, apparently stronger than him, snarled once before snapping his mouth over her and tearing into her flesh. Joey closed his eyes when Chris screamed, but his cat didn't let go. And when Chris finally fainted, Joey called out for his brother Nolan.

You don't need me. He told him that he thought he'd killed her. He didn't really think that, but he wanted Nolan to come help him. *Is she naked right now? I mean, I'm assuming that she is. Do you want me there to see that? Besides, I think she's right in having you do this. I was going to suggest it myself.*

I cannot wait until you meet your own mate. I hope she's human and has no idea what we are, and runs screaming in the night. His brother laughed, and Joey told him to be quiet. *I hear it. Her heart is...it's getting stronger.*

Of course is it. I told you she'd be fine. That girl is going to give you a run for your money, big brother. And your children are going to be horrible little brats. Who I will watch whenever you need me to so I can teach them everything I know. Joey laughed this time, feeling better all the time. *When you do finish this, come to see me in my office. I'll make sure she's okay and having no ill effects. I doubt she will, but I can look her over for you.*

After thanking his brother, he moved away from Chris. Shifting back into his human self, he pulled on his clothing while he kept an eye on her. She was simply the most beautiful creature he'd ever seen. And Joey was more in love with her with every beat of his heart than he ever thought possible.

When he was sure that she was all right, he picked her up and took her to his car. He was going to have to get her one as well soon. And her things would be brought here from her apartment. Allen said he'd go back and pack things up once they were finished with the lawsuit against the other firm. He was never going to have to worry about money again.

Once home, he carried her up to their room. Carol told him she'd fix him a tray, and if she was surprised by the fact that Chris was unconscious, she didn't act like it. Joey laid her gently on the bed and tried to think what to put on her after he cleaned her up. The blood nearly made him sick.

"I've taken one of your shirts from the dryer, sir. She'll be nice and warm in it." Carol stood next to the bed and then looked at him. "I'm just going to use a wee bit of magic to dress her. No point in making her all sore, too, from moving her about."

In seconds, less really, not only was Chris in his shirt but her hair was pulled back in a ponytail and she was under the covers. Carol, true to her word, had him a tray brought up ten minutes later with enough food for three people. Joey only ate a little of it. He was too worried to bother with it.

After Carol came up and took the tray, tisking at him for not keeping his strength up, he moved to the bed to lay down with Chris. He could hear her heart beating as well as his was, and felt better for it. But he was still terrified at what he'd done. And what he'd taken on in such a short amount of time.

There were four more horses coming in next week. One of them might need to be put down, Davey had told them. She had suffered terribly since birth and was treated like a monster. The loss of her foal had simply sent her over the edge. Then there was the thing with Jackson. He was going to come here and try to kill his mate, and then take whatever magic she had. Micah was going to be worked on magically to remove Angel's magic that had been stored in him for Chris.

You're thinking too hard. Stop it. Joey smiled at his mom's advice. *I can almost feel it down here. And I wasn't snooping, but I know when one of my children are hurt. What do you think will happen when that man gets here? You have it all worked out in your head, so tell me.*

He's going to come here with his guns blazing and I think he's going to expect her to be…I don't know, easy. She might have been before all this — not just me changing her, but with everything that is going on. Chris is much stronger than she was when she came here to find Micah, don't you think? Mom told him that she knew she was stronger. *I love her very much.*

Of course you do. So do I. At least she doesn't call me Miss Gracie. I thought I would have to brain Reggie before she stopped doing that. He felt his mom's laughter, and he smiled again. *Joey, what are you going to do with those ponies? Some of them, from what Tony told me, might be dangerous.*

We're going to give them a second chance. It might be their last, but we're going to try. She told him that was a good name. *Name? I don't understand.*

You're a rancher now, aren't you? Both you and Chris are going to work to get justice for these animals, and your ranch needs a name. Second Chances is as good as any. He told her he liked it. *Good; now go to sleep. Didn't your grandda always tell you that things always look worst in the middle of the night? And that by the bright of the day, you wonder why you worried?*

He did. Joey rolled over, and Chris moved closer to him. It was a wonderful way to let his worries move away. *Mom, I don't tell you this enough, but I really do love you. I don't know what we would have done without you all these years.*

You would have survived, as I have done. But with grandbabies and new blood in the family, I'm finding that getting up every day is a good deal easier. Your father would have been so proud of all of you. She told him she loved him. *Now go to sleep, young man. It's going to be a long day tomorrow, and we need to be on our toes.*

Joey closed his eyes. He let go of as much of his thoughts as he could, but some were there until he could work them out. But when Chris laid her head on his chest, things suddenly didn't seem that bad any more.

~~~

Chris woke in the big bed alone. She could hear the shower running and thought about going in there to see if she could get Joey to scrub her back. Getting out of the bed, she moved to the large room and had a sudden thought. What if it wasn't him? But then why would someone use his shower in his room? Sneaking into the room, this time with the sheet around her body, she was relieved to find Joey there and not someone else.

Dropping the sheet, she reached for the door just as he turned. She could see that he was upset about something, but she had no idea what. Before she could ask, he pulled her to him and held her. When he sobbed, she felt her own heart break.

"Emmett." She nodded, not sure what he was saying, but knew that something had happened to the big vampire. "He was killed this morning. His house was...it caught fire when one of the houses next to his burned. I told him to move to the country."

Chris held Joey while he cried. She knew few men that would do that, and loved and respected him all the more because he'd been willing to do this with her there. He started telling her what had happened as she held him.

"He called out for me. I thought it was...I really had no idea what he was doing, but he screamed out in pain before he started talking. The house had fallen in on him and he said that he was dying." Chris nodded, thinking of her own sister saying the same words to her. "I told him I was coming to him, but he said it was much too late. But that he left me everything, and if I didn't make it worth something for him, he'd come back and haunt me. He was my best friend."

"I know. I really liked him too." She had too. He was a very old-world gentleman, and she had enjoyed talking to him. "What can we do? We should go there. Perhaps he was mistaken and he's going to be okay."

"A stake...one of the beams hit him in the chest. He's gone." Chris nodded and watched as Joey turned off the water and reached for a towel. "I'm sorry. How are you feeling? Mom thought you'd be down for a few more days."

"I feel wonderful." She did too. But she didn't tell him just how wonderful she felt because she knew that he was hurting too. "I'm very hungry. Are you hungry?"

"Not really." She'd noticed the tray of untouched food when she'd come in here with him. "I guess you'd like to take a shower. I'm going to go down to the office for a little while."

"How about you scrub my back?" Chris had no idea how to be a seductress, but she did reach for him. "I need you. I know that my timing could be better, but I'm nearly jumping out of my skin with need."

Joey pulled her body to his. He was still warm and wet from the shower, and she loved the way her hands slid over his body when he kissed her. As he lifted her up and pressed her against the warm tile, she moaned when his cock moved against her pussy.

"I would love nothing more than to eat you right now." She begged him to do it. "When I do, I want you to scream as loud as you can. I want to feel your climax too."

It wasn't hard for her to tell him she'd do just what he asked. But when he slid down her body after standing her on her feet, she felt every bite, every kiss as he marked her. Before he touched his mouth to her pussy, she'd come once already.

There was no build up as he sucked her clit into his mouth. When he bit down, not hard but none too gently either, she screamed. And when something moved along her skin, she looked down at her body and saw her cat; the black silky fur of her cat was making herself known.

"I want to take you in the woods today and run you down as my cat." Nodding, she felt her cat agree. "Then when I find you, I'm going to fuck you like an animal before my cat takes your pussy again."

"Please, Joey. I need you to take me. Please." He stood up. Chris leaned in and licked her juices from his face as he lifted her up again. This time he didn't kiss her as he slammed himself into her, but watched her face, as if he was trying to see into her soul. Grabbing onto his shoulders, Chris let him take her. His emotions were as strong as each of his thrusts. When he came, he leaned into her throat and bit her, tearing at her flesh like he'd been trying to tear it from her. Her cat, not to be outdone, shifted in her body so that when she bit Joey, Chris knew that it was just as painful for him.

He held her to him as he panted. His body, his cock was still deep inside of her, but she knew that he was spent. She was too. All she wanted to do was crawl back in the bed with him and sleep the day away. But when he lifted his head, she knew that wasn't going to be possible.

"Micah said for us to get our asses downstairs." Chris asked him if he knew what they'd been doing. "More than likely. He's newly mated too. I, however, would like to just stay here, buried deep inside of you until the world realizes that we're not going to participate anymore."

"I think that's a wonderful plan. Let's just do it your way." He laughed, and Chris smiled back at him. "I love you. I'm so glad that we did this. I feel amazing."

"I'm glad we did as well. But we might have to grovel to Micah. He's our new leader now, and he's taking his job a little too seriously. Grandda retired last month, and Micah has been spouting rules at us that we're breaking right and left." He reached for a towel and handed it to her. "I think he might calm down a little, but he wants to do a good job."

"I don't know the rules yet, but if he gives me a hard time, I'll change him into a toad." Joey asked her if she could really do that. "I have no idea, but it would be a good threat, don't you think?"

Joey helped her dry off and she did the same for him. As they moved into their bedroom, she noticed that the bed had been made as well as the tray was gone. Someone had been in here while they'd been…she looked at Joey.

"It's not what you think." She nodded at him, wondering what he meant. "No one came in here. I don't know what does it, but whenever I leave a room, no matter how messy I make it, when I come back to it, everything is neat and tidy. Even a towel on the floor is picked up and replaced with a clean dry one. It's a little freaky to get used to. I meant to ask Carol about it, but to be honest, she sort of scares me a little."

"Me too." There was fresh clothing in her drawers too. Not only her things from the apartment, but new things as well. Sexy little things that she'd never have bought for herself, but was really excited to wear. When she pulled out a pair of jeans, again not hers, she noticed that they'd been laundered as well as folded the way she usually did her pants. She asked Joey if he had the same things.

"My suits are still in the closet where I had them, but there are more shirts. And there are some with…Mom and I talked about this ranch and a name for it last night, just as a joke. Now I have shirts with the name on them. Several of them, as a matter of fact."

Chris went to her closet. There were a variety of shirts in her size with the name Second Chances on them, with pictures of Elwood. Pulling one over her head, tears filling her eyes, she looked at Joey.

"This is the best thing…I love it. And Elwood is…I'm so…I don't know what to say. Second Chances is going to be…oh, Joey." He held her while she cried. She was so happy she didn't want to go downstairs at all, but to hide up here with the wonderful feelings she was having right now. "Tell them to go away. I want to just be held by you."

"There are horses coming today." That had her lifting her head. "I thought you'd still be resting when they arrived, but you are never going to do things the way people expect, are you?"

As if he'd deemed it, there was a noise in the yard and they both went to the window. Three large semis were there, and each of them were pulling an animal trailer. She grabbed his hand and they ran down the stairs. This was much better than anything she'd been planning today.

Micah stood up when they entered the kitchen. "Don't know what you want, but right now, I need this. And so does Joey." He looked like he was going to say more, but she moved out of the kitchen and into the yard. Micah followed them.

The first truck had two horses in it. She helped them unload by staying out of the way. Joey made fun of her because she had wanted to knock the big man out of the way that was pulling down the ramp and do it herself. He was just taking too long. But when they were unloaded and put into the barn, she walked to the next one. Joey was right beside her.

"She's not well." Chris had no idea why but she could feel the young mare's pain. "Her foal died last spring and she didn't take it well. They've been doing nothing for her since she has turned on them. I want you to know that Heath is on his way here in the event that she needs to be dealt with."

"You mean put her down." He nodded. "No. We can't do that to her. She needs a chance with us."

The trailer was left for last as they moved to the third one. It had two small horses in it, as well as a donkey. Chris looked at Joey, who shrugged. They had not been told he was coming apparently.

"Wouldn't leave the other horse." The driver started into the trailer and moved back when the horse, a gray one, reared up at him. "She's a bit mad at me still, I guess. I had to…I didn't hurt her none, but she's mad because it took us so long to make a deal about the donkey. She wasn't going nowhere without him."

Chris wanted to go in and bring them both out, but the driver, a big burly man, said he'd do it. For all his size, Chris was impressed with how gentle he was when he spoke to the horse.

"Come on now, you want to make a good first impression, don't ya? Come out on of there and let the pretty lady get a look at you. She won't be taking away your friend." The horse snorted at him. "You can be mad at me all you want, but this here woman is going to give you what you want. More'n them others would."

"What did they do to her?" The driver glanced at Joey before looking at her. "I need to know so we don't make the same mistakes."

"They bred her too young is what they did. Messed her up in her innards. Poor thing…she's not got what it takes no more to do more than fight ya. I'm thinking they meant to put her down, but that notice that came out that you were helping them horses out had me going back there and making them a deal." Chris looked at Joey, who seemed just as surprised as she was about the notice. "Cost me a might more than I could do, but I wasn't going to have her put down, not this beauty."

"I'll pay you back, every cent. For the donkey too." The man nodded at Joey when he spoke, and Chris wondered how much it had been. But then the donkey moved up to her and put his head under her hand.

The horse watched her. When she started moving toward her, the driver warned her not to make any sudden moves. But when she put her hand out, waiting for the small head to touch it, she felt tears fill her eyes when she realized how terrified the little thing was. As soon as her head touched her hand, Chris felt it all.

"She's depressed. Very much so. The donkey made her eat and kept her from dying when he stopped eating too. She calls him Baby." The other pony, a white one, came forward as well, and she realized they were twins. "This one is going to have a foal, and she's afraid. But she won't leave her sister."

As they were helped out of the trailer, the last one was opened. Chris saw Heath getting out of his car just as the trailer rocked. The horse was beating the sides of it with not just her hooves, but her head as well. Chris didn't go inside, but she could still feel the poor thing.

"She's...she's hurting. Not just her body, but her head too. There's something there." Heath asked her what it was. "I don't know. It's...I think she has a tumor."

"Yeah, I thought so. Got her paperwork last night and was surprised that nobody checked on that. Olivia, that's her name, was the daughter of a couple of prime flesh, but she never came around. I'd bet she was born with that thing and now it's more than likely too late for her." Chris hated to admit it, but she thought so too. "You're going to have to make the decision, sweetie. I can do the job, but not without you giving me the okay."

In the end Joey had to sign off on the paperwork. Olivia never came out of the trailer, and Heath had to go inside and do it there. When it was over, Chris went into the house. Reggie met her at the living room door with the babies. Chris took them both and sat down on the couch and cried for an hour.

Chapter 9

"I don't understand what you're telling me. There is plenty of money in that account, and the charge card is a company credit card. There should be no problems with that." The clerk at the hotel desk only stared at him. Jackson was ready to scream, but he was trying his best to hold his temper. "Look, why don't you call my firm? I have the number right here."

"We did call them, Mr. Hill. They told us that as of now, this credit card is no longer being honored on their end. Perhaps you should call them." When she walked away from him, Jackson started to tell her to get her ass back here, he wasn't finished with this. But the appearance of Myra made him move away. He nearly tripped over his luggage.

"You did this, didn't you?" Myra laughed and sat down on the couch. Jackson had no choice but to sit by her. Today she was dressed all in purple, including her hair. And it wasn't just purple, but a neon sort of color that made him think of black lights and spinning balls. "Why is my checking account drained, as well as my company card no longer useful?"

"You've been fired, I'm afraid." He told her she was lying. "I don't lie, and you have been. There was a little problem with your billing. You should know better than to cheat a system that relies on you to be honest. They caught you with your pants down, so to speak."

"So, I padded the time I spent with clients. They all do that." She shook her head. "Yes they do. I bet your buddy Chris does it as well."

"Actually, she under bills her clients. The firm knows that, and they don't mind a few hours off here and there. But apparently it was noticed that some of the times that you had billed Mr. Pinkerton, he was dead." Jackson tried to remember if he'd even known that he was dead. "He died over a month ago. You've been billing him over twenty hours a week since then. I don't think you have that much power that you can speak to the dead and then bill them."

"So. It's not like his estate can't afford it." She only nodded. "What else is going on? They don't fire you for one little overbilling."

"Chris quit, did she tell you that? Gave her notice just the other day. The place was heartbroken about it. But her reasons for leaving might not have gone over well with the partners. I don't think that she cared for you telling her clients that you and she were an item. And then there was the added fact that she's getting married to a fine lawyer." Myra leaned back and Jackson wanted to strangle her. "You do and I will not just get your powers, but I will not let you go easily."

He had to take several deep calming breaths before he could speak. Things were not just going sour right now, but he had expenses that he couldn't fix. The hotel was kicking him out...had kicked him out by packing up for him. The money that he'd been using, his money, was now gone, and his account was overdrawn by not just a few dollars, but thousands the woman had told him this morning when he'd called to have a wire transfer. And now Myra was telling him that he'd lost his fucking job too.

"Okay. That explains the credit card, but not my account. I have well over six grand in there. Did they take that as well?" He was still reeling about Chris. The nerve of her getting him into trouble with his job. He didn't like it, but that was no reason for her to bite him in the ass about it. It was then that he remembered Myra telling him something about him owing her money. "How much did you take?"

"All of it. And it wasn't nearly enough. I usually charge ten thousand for the murder of one of my creatures. Did you know that they're mine? I mean, I created them, and when someone uses them I get a settlement from that. But when they're killed...well, I take what I can. Same as you." She waved her hand over her outfit and it changed from the purple to a blinding green. He was stunned to see her hair had changed as well. "You need to make some arrangements to pay the rest, or I'll have to think you're not going to pay. And that simply won't do."

He had some money in an offshore account. Not a great deal, but enough for him to get a start once this thing with Chris was finished. Jackson didn't have high standards of living, but the money was not going to last very long if he owed Myra another four grand for a thing that hadn't done its job in the first place. Jackson needed to get this over with so he could move on with his other plans.

"As you well know, I don't have it. And as of right now I'm penniless, as well as without a place to stay while I'm here. I can pay you some of what I owe you when I deal with Chris." Myra laughed, and he looked at her. "You still think that she's stronger than me, don't you? Well, she's not. Not only does her power lay dormant, but she has no base in the first place. Angel had it all."

"You do what you think you should. If she kills you, please remember that I told you so." She stood up then, and he looked around to see if anyone had noticed that she was now dressed in a formal gown of the most hideous shade of yellow he'd ever seen. "I have a dinner to attend. I'm going to have fun and think of you while I'm enjoying myself. You might want to make sure that all your ducks are in a row, Jackson. I don't think you'll have many opportunities once you make your way to Chris's house."

Then she just disappeared. Jackson sat there for another ten minutes. If asked, he couldn't have said what he'd been thinking about for his life, but he did get up when the clerk at the counter said his name.

"I'm sorry, sir, but we don't allow loitering. I'm afraid you'll have to move on." He started to ask her where the hell he was supposed to go but only picked up his bags. The first thing he was going to have to do was find a bank, then transfer some of his cash to his account. Hopefully he could do this without Myra taking it as soon as it hit. This thing was not turning out the way he'd hoped.

Calling the firm had gotten him nowhere. He was informed that his last check would go to covering the added expense of the court costs from the Pinkerton estate. Then he was asked how he was going to have his things shipped to his home.

"You mean the stuff in my desk?" The woman at the other end told him that was correct. "Why can't I just come by when I get home and pick it up? I can't really afford the shipping right at this moment."

"Oh no, sir. You are no longer allowed on the premises. Security knows to make sure that you cannot enter the building as well. We'll have to ship it to you. How would you like to pay for that? We'd prefer that you used a major credit card please, and things will not go out until we're assured of getting the money." He hung up on her.

There was no talking to some people. They had a script and they never deviated from it, no matter what. He called her kind cattle. Some day he was going to have the power to change those kind of beings into just what they were. A herd of cattle. His phone ringing startled him to stop walking.

"Hello, Jackson. Are you having a bit of trouble?" Chris. He should have known that Myra would run to her to let her know what was going on. "I understand that you've been let go from the firm. I guess you really didn't like the job anyway, did you?"

"I like you even less. Were you in on this with her? With Myra? If so, I'm going to make it my life to ruin you. And that new husband of yours. Does he know what you are, Chris? Have you shared your life with him and all of the truth? You told me that you had, but I just don't believe he'd be that understanding." She laughed. "You won't think this is so funny when I have your sister's magic. I'm going to make you pay."

"I don't think so, but you're more than welcome to come here and try. Oh, but you don't have a car or money. Would you like for me to send you a car? I could you know, just send you a limo to pick you up." Jackson would rather die, and he told her that. "Too bad. But I have made some arrangements for you. There's a cute little bed and breakfast right near where you're standing. Do you see it? It's called the Bustle. I'm not sure why, but there you have it."

"And what is this place really? A falling down building that will land on my head once I enter it? Why the hell would you think that I'd trust you after yesterday?" He'd been sick for nearly three hours. Every time he thought of what she'd done to him, he was throwing up all over again.

"It's really a B&B, Jackson. Look it up on your phone while you can." He moved to the side of the street that the building was on and went to the Internet. He rarely used this thing for looking things up on, but he was desperate to find a place he could stay. "I just asked Joey and he said that it's called that because the woman who owned it before it was converted used to sell bustles. I guess there are some of her designs in every room."

Jackson was surprised when it came up on his phone. "Why are you being nice to me? Is it because you think I'm going to go easy on you? I'm not. I want what is mine, Chris, and you'd do well to remember who is stronger here." Her laughter rattled over the phone, and he waited for her to finish. "What do I have to do to stay here? And this had better not be another one of your jokes."

Jackson had thought about her ability to have him see what he had yesterday. He had no idea why she'd do this to him, but he had a feeling that Myra was involved. She could make those things happen a lot easier than Chris could have. Not to mention, there was no way she could have done it without being close to him. Jackson could work his magic at a distance, but not much more than about ten feet. He was hoping that would improve as well.

"I'm working on being nice. Not to you, but you're down on your luck and I'm going to help you. With this. You can stay in the place for a week, but after that, you're on your own. Oh, and don't bother with the overseas account. Myra has donated it to a very good cause. She said to tell you thanks." The line was dead before he could tell her what he thought of her or Myra.

Jackson stood outside for twenty minutes. He was afraid to go in if he was honest with himself. For all he knew, Myra could have it so that once he entered, his powers would be gone and he'd never be able to leave. Things were not going the way he'd hoped they would since coming here. But he needed a place to rest. A place he could plan for his confrontation with Myra and Chris.

As soon as he was in his room, he went around testing his magic on it. Not a lot but enough to let him know that this place was real. He wasn't sure he would ever eat again, but he was comfortable for now. Leaning back on the massive headboard, Jackson thought of the rules he'd learned to live by the hard way.

The number one rule was not to harm another witch. You could kill them so long as their power was stronger than yours, but you couldn't maim or harm them for self-gain. He had wondered if what Myra had done to him yesterday counted, and was pretty sure that making one sick wasn't really maiming anyone. That was a weird rule, but it had served him well over the last few years in that he followed it to the letter.

Secondly, and most important of all the rules he'd learned, was to never use magic on yourself. Ever. He'd done that only one time, and had vowed that no matter what, he'd never do it again.

The day had been shitty. Not just shitty now that he thought about it, but really in the whole down in the dump kind of day where you wished yourself dead. Jackson had had no job, no money, and he was struggling to make it to the end of the week with what little food he'd had left. All he'd wanted was a hot pizza. He didn't even care if it was just cheese, just a hot one with steam rolling off the top of it. So in a fit of what he thought of now as stupidity, he'd made someone bring him one.

It had arrived within minutes of his request. The man seemed to be slightly confused when he handed him a bottle of water in form of payment, but he had his food and he slammed the door in his face before he could ask any questions. Jackson sat the hot box on the table and gathered up what he thought he'd need to enjoy the first hot meal he'd had in days.

"I should have known better." Speaking aloud made him wince at the sound, but he thought more of the disaster. And there were more descriptive words for what had happened, but he was okay with disaster for now.

His plate was in his hand, and there was another bottle of water there for his own drink. Napkins had been placed just so, and even though they were from various restaurants he'd been to over the last months, it mattered little to the grand dinner he was about to have.

Then he opened the box.

He was never really sure how he'd sat in the chair. He was just suddenly seated. The dinner that he'd been looking forward to stared back at him. Literally. The face that was made of the hot cheese sort of melted together, and the eyes, if that was what there were, seemed to blink in and out of focus.

"This is wrong. You know that, right?" He nodded at the cheesy face. "Yeah, I thought you did. But you did it anyway, didn't you?"

"I'm hungry." On some level he knew that he was having a conversation with an inanimate object, but he thought his mind had gone out for a break by this point. "I just wanted to have something good for a change."

"So you thought 'I have some power, I'll just conjure myself some dinner. To eat by myself. For my own entertainment.'" Jackson remembered nodding. "No. You can't do that. You were told this, and yet here you are about to eat a part of me. Would you like a little of my chin? How about my cheek? There's a nice piece of basil at my mouth there. Would you like to nibble on that? Or my eyes? Do you want to eat my eyes, Jackson?"

The plate in his hand had shattered on the floor. The thing, the pizza man, just kept taunting him, offering up parts of himself for Jackson to eat. Instead, Jackson closed up the box and put the pie, along with his stack of napkins, in front of the apartment across from him. He didn't even look to see if it had been taken in after a brief knock on the door. Jackson had never eaten a piece of pizza or anything that even resembled one since then.

Stripping down, he took a long shower. He was exhausted, he realized, and he had a longer day tomorrow. He wondered briefly if he should have taken Chris up on her offer to bring him to her home, but all he could think about now was sleep. So he laid down on the bed naked and closed his eyes. Tomorrow would be better. It just had to be.

~~~

"Tell me again why I'm calling him and taunting him?" Micah had had her call him twice now to mess with him.

The food idea had actually been Reggie's. Some days she wondered where that girl's mind went. Of course the food had been perfectly fine both before and after he'd eaten it, but she made him believe it was bad, and that had been what was worth it. She supposed that in a small way she was enjoying this a little too much.

"Pissed off people make the most mistakes." Chris asked Micah what he meant. "When you're upset, how rational are you? Do you ever make sound decisions or are they off the cuff, usually half assed?"

"Terrible ones, as a matter of fact. But he didn't seem upset, just...I guess he just sounded more resolved in that he was going to get me back." Micah nodded. "Okay, so I have to piss him off because I want him to be stupid in his coming here. You think that...you and the rest of the family think that I can take him. You do know that I can't, right? I'm not that good of a witch."

Myra came into the room then. The woman was the most color matched person she'd ever met. Each time she saw her everything was the same color from the top of her head, hair included, to the bottom of her shoes. Today she was all in pink, a violent shade that reminded her of that stuff she used to drink as a kid when her belly was upset.

Chris had been dropped off at Micah's home when Joey had gone into town to talk to Emmett's employees. There was a will and it would be read in a few days, but Paul had asked him to come in and talk to them. Joey asked her to come here so he'd not have to worry about her when she decided that she didn't want to go into town.

"Can you tell me how you knew that Olivia had a tumor?" Chris felt the pain of her death again. And she didn't want to answer Myra. "I'm sorry, but I want you to think about that. And the way that Elwood is attached to you when he won't allow anyone else near him."

"Joey can touch him." Micah only nodded and Myra giggled. "I don't understand any of this."

"You're using your magic, dear. And doing a very good job of it too." Chris shook her head, and both Micah and Myra started to nod as Myra continued. "You're very powerful. Extremely so. And your mother did you both an injustice as well as kept you safe when she told you that you and your sister were not strong. It is more than likely the only thing that kept you from being killed all those years ago."

"How would you know this? I mean, you didn't know my mom. How do you know what she did for us?" Myra told her it was in her mark. And that she did know her mother, as well as her grandmother. Chris pulled her sleeve up and showed it to her. "You mean this? I've had this...well, not this particular one, but this mark had been here since before I knew I was different by having it."

"Yes. Angel had one as well. Not as dark as yours, right?" Chris nodded. "Nor your mother's. Hers was much darker and wider than your sisters, but your mom would have known what you were the moment that she conceived you. A very powerful and extremely sought after witch. One that would take on things that no one else, not even me, would be able to do. Like I said, she was a good woman, your mother, but she was never very smart when it came to the magic that ran through your veins and the rest of your family's."

"She was brilliant. And she said we were not worthy of the look of the council. We were...she told us to hide what we were from everyone so that we'd not be burned at the stake like…well, like our ancestors were." Myra nodded and smiled at her. "You knew as well, didn't you?"

"Oh yes. It was my idea to hide you away. Your father, he was a great warlock; not a witch like Jackson is, but an honest to goodness warlock. His death, his murder, was something that hurt us for years. More years than we would have thought it would. As soon as I found out about his death and the circumstances, I went to your mother. She agreed that if they knew what you were, and even Angel to a point, then they would come for you as well."

"And now they are coming for us. At least one is." Myra told her that he would be the first of many should she not use it, and now. "You mean to kill Jackson. I don't think I can do that."

"He's not going to leave you much of a choice, I'm afraid." Myra patted her hand before continuing. "And if you don't, not only will your mate be hurt, but many more can and will die because of him and his greed."

Chris wasn't sure about that. In fact, other than her love for Joey, she wasn't sure about a lot of things. But when the phone rang again and Micah answered, she knew that Jackson was in the bed and breakfast and that things were going to start happening now.

Chapter 10

Joey watched the horses. There were ten of them now, and he wasn't sure how many more were coming in the coming days. The hands that he had hired on Davy's say-so had told him that he was going to need more room, and just like that, the barn seemed to grow. Joey had come out here to learn how to breathe again. When someone stood next to him, he looked over at his grandda when he laughed.

"You're a might on the tense side, boy. Anything I can help you figure out?" Joey had no idea where to even begin to ask for help and told him that. "Yeah, I can see you trying your best to keep on top of stuff. But you can't, so you might as well just go with it."

"I'm not a go with it sort of person." He thought of the barn. "Mike, the new hand, came to me about an hour ago and said that we'd need a bigger barn. And that we'd need to figure out where to store the grain and other things we were going to need to keep the horses fed and healthy. I went in with him, and both of us just stared at the new addition. Do you know what Mike did? He thanked me."

"Right polite of him if you ask me. Did you want him to hit you or something?" Joey shook his head. "Then what has them underwear of yours all twisted up? You needed it, and right there it was."

"Grandda, the barn moved to accommodate my needs. And I don't think Chris did it." Grandda laughed again. "This is not funny. I think I did that. And...and we now have a stock barn. I had no idea what a stock barn was until Andy came and asked me if he could have a lock for it. Said people might think that it was free should they know how much stock we have in it."

"Did you have one for him?" Joey nodded, not caring at all for the humor that lit his grandda's face. "Well, then. Problem solved. Again. You're looking at this all wrong, son. You have to think how much this is helping them poor ponies."

"They don't care." His grandda started to tell him they sure did when Joey cut him off, "No, I mean they don't care that I'm a panther or that Chris is one. They come to us like we've raised them from foals. That's just not right either."

"Again, I don't think you're going about this right. You wanted a ranch, there you have it. You got yourself a pretty mate, and she is one pretty mate. Smart too. Not that Reggie isn't, but you gotta admit that it sure is nice talking business with your mate and she has an idea what the heck you're talking about." Grandda and he watched as Elwood and two of the pretty fillies danced and played across the field. "Joey, my boy, there ain't nothing finer than a woman who loves you. The magic is...well, it's not something I know a lot about, but it's there and you might as well make some good of it."

"Myra said that we'd be stronger once we have what Micah's holding. I'm not sure what we're going to do with more when we can barely handle what we have." Grandda laughed again. "Keep it up, old man, and I'm going to tell Grandma that you're sneaking over here to eat Carol's pies and cakes."

"You won't do that to your old grandda, will you?" Joey nodded, knowing full well that Grandma already knew and that he'd not had to tell her. "She's got it in her head that I'm going to keel over soon and them babies won't have me around to show them a thing or two. I told her…well, I didn't actually tell her straight out, but I did want to tell her that I think me being on a diet is as foolish as it comes. She can be a tad on the mean side when she has her froth up."

Joey laughed now. Everyone, including him, was slightly afraid of the women in this family. His mom was the best woman in the world, but she could make him feel less than an ant with just a look. And Grandma could have him whimpering when she just cocked that pretty brow of hers. Joey hated, as much as his brothers did, to disappoint them. He was sure his grandda did as well.

The noise behind them had them both turning. He had no idea who the man was standing there with his hat in his hands, but Joey felt his cat stir along his skin. Not in a way that made him think that this man was trouble, but in a way that made him think he was someone he knew.

"You Joey Bentley? The lawyer that is giving animals a chance at life?" Joey nodded and felt his grandda move away. He wasn't sure what he was doing until he made his way to the house. Joey wasn't sure what the wolf in front of him wanted, but he was certainly down on his luck. "My name is Harry Barlow. I need me one too."

"One what?" Harry told him he needed a second chance too. "I'm sorry, but right now we have all the hands we can take on. If you are looking for work, there's a diner in town that my sister-in-law runs that helps—"

"Davey told me to come here. He said you might need me." Joey nodded, and the man took the last steps to him and put out his hand. "I'm a wolf. And Davey, he told me that I could maybe get myself a place to sleep at night and help you with the horses. I used to work on a big ranch down in Kentucky. They let me go when…the horses got spooked by another shifter and I was blamed for it."

Joey had no idea why he thought the man was telling him the truth, but he did. When Myra was standing beside him, Harry took a step back but said nothing. Joey wasn't sure he wanted to stand close to her either. Today she was dressed in what he could only think of as pus yellow. She smiled at Harry, then looked at Joey.

"No one can lie to you. I might have told you that before, but I forgot." Joey told her that it would be helpful to know these things before he needed them. "And what fun would that be for me?"

"I'm not gonna lie to you. Not now and not ever if you give me a chance." Joey had no idea what to do. He'd said that Davey had sent him. But where was he supposed to put…? He looked at Myra.

"There is a place for him, isn't there?" She just smiled. "You know, I don't think I like you very much. In fact…you kind of scare me too much for me to tell you just how I feel."

She touched her fingers to his cheek, and she smiled at him. "You're too tense. I'll take young Harry here to the bunk house. There might be one or two more coming in. You're going to need it. Oh, and please have Carol find a cook for them. I think it was very smart of you to have put in a large kitchen. Like I said, you're going to need it."

As "young" Harry followed her—the man had to be about the same age as his grandparents—his grandda came out of the house with Chris. She was laughing at something, and Joey had a feeling he'd told her what he was saying to him. Joey was going to have a long talk with Grandma, and he'd bet Grandda wouldn't be allowed to be on his own for the rest of his life.

"We have a bunk house. And more help." She nodded and told him Davey had called. "Did he happen to tell you how many more we're to expect before we're fully staffed?"

"Three more. Younger than Harry was—Grandda told me about him—but they're going to arrive when the new horses come. Three more, but all of them are healthy he told me." She wrapped her arms around him, and Joey felt better already. "I think we're going to need to work more just to afford all this. This isn't a cheap way to have a home."

"No. I don't want to alarm you or anything, but we might want to wait a while on any more. I'm not poor by any stretch of the imagination, but neither of us have any clients but a few horses, and they don't strike me as having a lot of disposable income either." Carol called him to the phone. "Whoever it is, I don't want to talk to them. Tell them…tell them you can't find me."

"I'm thinking you should take this." He didn't know why, but the sound of her voice had him moving to the house. She was holding the cordless out to him when he stepped to the back deck. "It's that Mr. Simmons person. He said that he thinks you should come back to the offices."

Joey took the phone and could hear something going on in the background. When Paul finally answered him, he sounded like he was drunk. It took Joey three tries to get him to calm down.

"Can I send you something? I mean, it's yours if you want it here or there, but I think...well, we'd all like for you to know what might be in it, so here would be fun. A crate, a big frigging crate, arrived for you just now." He giggled, not a sound Joey could ever remember hearing from the man. "Pardon my language, Joey, but this thing is fucking huge and it has to weigh a ton. Or maybe two. It's currently sitting on the back of a trailer, and there are...let me count them again. There are nine armed guards standing next to it."

Joey told Chris what Paul had just said. "Ask him if there is a name other than yours on it. Or an address. Surely one of the guards...you said that they're armed? Ask him to see if they know anything."

When Paul came back, he was no longer laughing but sounding sort of down. He told him it was from Emmett. "I'm going to just send it to you out there. We don't...it's too soon for us to see what he might have sent you. Is that okay?"

"Yes. Send it out. Do you know if the guards come with it, or are they just there for it?" Paul told him that until he signed for it, they were as much a part of it as the nails holding the crate together. "And you have no idea what it might be?"

"No. And whatever it is, you're going to need help getting it offloaded. I don't know what it might be, but I'm thinking that Emmett has to be laughing his ass off right now thinking of you getting this thing." Joey could imagine the big man doing just that. "Let us know what it is if it's not too personal. It's nice to know that he is taking care of you from the grave. The man loved you like a son. And I'm sure you returned it."

134

"I will. That's a promise. And I did love the man. He was like a second father to me." After he hung up, he told Chris and Carol what was going on. Carol told him that a cook had arrived at the bunk house and was currently stocking it. Joey didn't even ask. Stocking it with what, he wasn't sure he wanted to know anymore. He and Chris decided that they needed to get away, and he told Carol that they'd not be there for dinner.

"Good. I got things brewing for that man." Joey only nodded and moved to the stairs. He was pretty sure he didn't want to know what that meant either. But he did know that when Jackson got there, he was going to be in for a huge surprise.

~~~

After a second trip to the little shop, he realized that he'd been more than a fool. He'd been a gullible fool. Not only was the shop gone, but it looked as if it had never been there. And while the restaurant where he'd been poisoned was real, he didn't go in even for a glass of water. He had no idea what Myra was up to in doing this to him, but she was going to pay.

As he made his way back to the bed and breakfast, he walked to the little convenience store that wasn't far from him. He got himself a coffee only after he saw three people get some and enjoy it, and then he got a Danish that was plastic wrapped and had the longest expiration date on it. He wasn't taking any more chances with his belly.

Eating it as he walked, he tried to tell himself that this wasn't going to get him into trouble. Jackson wasn't worried about the council any more. He was going to be stronger than most of them anyway, and to his way of thinking, he'd gotten the magic from Angel fairly. They couldn't have any qualms about that either.

"You'd think that." Jackson stood up from the bench he was sitting on when the man appeared in front of him. He looked around, thinking that Myra was up to her tricks again, but the man laughed before he could say anything. "Myra is the least of your problems. You should be more worried about me and what I'm going to do with you."

"Me?" Jackson heard his voice squeak and felt stupid. It also made his temper, not in the best of form lately, rise up. "I don't worry about anyone. And if Myra thinks this is going to get her anywhere with me, like scaring me off, then she's got another think coming."

"Myra is, as I have said, the least of your problems. What do you think the grand witch is going to do when you get there? Say, here you go, take whatever you want and I'll be just as happy as I can be?" He shook his head. "No. She's going to pull up her considerable magic and blow your ass out of the hemisphere. And I'm going to still get what I want."

"Grand witch? There is...who the hell are you?" The man introduced himself, and Jackson thought the man a fool. "Well, Tyron, all I can say for you is that you'd better stay out of my way. Because when I get to Angel's magic, I'm going to be powerful beyond anything that has happened for a while. A long while."

"You think so? And who is Angel? The sister? That shit is gone for you. The grand witch has plans to take it from the cat today. And when she does, it will be over for most smaller witches like you. The only person that will be able to come anywhere near her power is a warlock. And that isn't you." Jackson started to tell him he was nuts when Tyron raised his hand. "Don't get yourself all twisted up. You are just a witch, while I'm a warlock. Do you have any idea of the difference between the two of us? How much more power I have than you? Why, I could kill you now and have yours too. But I won't. I need you."

Jackson sat down when he was told to. He had a feeling it was more of a command than a simple request, and he was sure the man had used magic to get him to do it. His body felt weighted down, his head fuzzy with…it felt as if he was being mind raped. And he didn't care for it.

"What are you talking about?" Jackson finally got his mouth to work right enough to ask. "There hasn't been a grand witch around for centuries. At least since before Myra took over the council. And you should know that they've disavowed me too." The chair that appeared under the man just as he was in the sitting position impressed Jackson. It looked more comfortable than his bed at home. "And why do you think I'd help you? I have my own plans."

"And they suck. You really think that you're going to go out to their ranch and simply take the magic that no longer belongs to you? And what do you think her husband is going to do? Just let you?"

Jackson had forgotten about the husband. He was still amazed by that. So far as he knew, she'd never even dated. Chris certainly never gave him the time of day, and he was one of her kind. Not just a witch, but an attorney too.

"Who is the grand witch?" Tyron just rolled his eyes. "Are you talking about Myra? I don't think…she's pretty powerful, but she's not—"

"Are you this fucking stupid all the time? If so, it's small wonder that you lost your job. Chris is the grand witch, you moron. She's been one since birth." Jackson shook his head. There was no way. "She's been dormant. Keeping herself safe, I would imagine, but once she met her cat, her match in all things, it came to light. And it really came to light. Not only is she the grand witch, but she might just be the most powerful one that has ever been born. And her husband? Christ, the man has no idea what his powerbase is, and he's just coming into it."

"Cat? What the hell are you talking about?" The man stood up and so did Jackson. But as soon as Tyron showed him what he was, the power that did indeed vibrate off him, Jackson had the overwhelming urge to bow down before him. He barely managed to keep himself from doing just that.

"Her mate is a cat. A panther. Joseph Bentley. Perhaps you might have heard of him. He is one of the most powerful and influential attorneys in the country. And one of the richest, thanks to his former boss and friend leaving him everything when he died this week." Tyron laughed, but it was bitter and cold. "Who knew that a vampire who had reached such an age as him could die in a house fire that wasn't even set to kill him?"

"Wait. Just wait. You're saying that my Chris is more than just a lower grade witch, that she's the grand witch of all. And her husband, this Bentley person, is rich and a panther? I just don't think you have your information straight. At the most, Chris is a level five or a six, but a grand? And a panther would have been run out of town before being trusted as an attorney with anyone. I don't think even a vampire would have anyone coming to him to use as one. How would he even make it to court? Those are daytime activities. Are you sure you have it all right?" Jackson felt himself being tossed away. His back hit the tree hard enough that he heard bones break before he felt them. "Please...."

Jackson watched Tyron come toward him. There would be nothing he could to do stop him from finishing the job;

Jackson knew as surely as he was now laying on the ground that he was dead. It was difficult for him to breathe, his head felt...he was dizzy, he was sick to his stomach. He could even see that his legs were bent at horrible angles, and he could no longer feel anything but his mouth.

"You fool." Jackson would have to agree with that assessment of himself. Tyron was right, he was a fool for fucking with a man like this one. "I need your help or I would simply let the buzzards pick at your bones. Anyone who came along could take your wallet."

Almost as quickly as he'd been hurt, he was standing up, his body now feeling better than it had in days. He looked at Tyron and wondered if he would show him how he'd done that. Then he realized that to ask would more than likely get him hurt again. But this time, there would be no one to heal him.

When Tyron told him that they were going to talk, Jackson nodded. He'd do whatever he was told, when he was told, and that was it. At least until he could get Angel's power and take this man out. Because no matter what he said, there was no way that Chris was the grand of anything. The woman could barely light a candle as far as he knew.

"You will call her. Have her invite you to the house. When you are invited, you'll call to me and tell me when." Jackson nodded and told him he'd have to wait on her to call him, he didn't have her number. "I have it, and you will as well before I leave here."

Jackson looked around and only just then realized they were no longer outside of the bed and breakfast, but in a nice hotel room. The large bed was made and looked as if someone had sat down on just the corner recently. He wasn't a neat person himself, but the seat imprint bothered him more than he could say.

"Are you listening to me?" Jackson looked at Tyron and nodded. He hadn't been and had to work hard not to glance at the bed again and again. "When you get there, you'll summon me. Just say my name and tell me to come to you. You know how to do that, right?"

"I do. But I had no idea that warlocks could be called the same way."

Tyron didn't even bother answering him but went on about the plan. "Once I'm there, you'll stay out of my way. I'll have to...never mind, but you'll get what you have coming to you. This I promise you. When do you think you can arrange this?" Jackson told him that as soon as he had the number and a phone, he'd call her. "Good. Then do it now. Try to arrange it so that it happens tomorrow. Or the next day. I want this over with."

"What are your plans for Chris?" Jackson still didn't think the man knew what he was talking about, but he'd play along. So long as he got what he had coming to him, the other man could do whatever he wanted.

"You let me worry about her and that mate of hers. Once I have what I want, no one will be able to take from me again. And Myra will be the first one I take care of." Jackson reminded him about his promise and that he'd get what he wanted. "You'll get what you have coming to you. For this I make you a promise. Just get me to the house and inside. You have to be inside when you summon me or it will not be worth it for you."

"And why do you have to be in the house?"

But Jackson was talking to air. And he had been returned to his room at the B&B. Lying next to the phone was a small dark piece of paper, and on it was a number written in white. Jackson, for some reason, found himself not wanting to pick it up, and called the number without touching it. When someone answered, Jackson had a terrible thought.

This could be another trick of Myra's.

Chapter 11

Nolan wasn't thrilled with this. He knew that should anything go wrong that he was right there to help, but since he had not one clue what might happen, much less go wrong, he was a little afraid for his big brother.

"You are not to touch him unless it is necessary for his life. If you do so, then it would transfer some of the magic that comes from him to you. And as we have no way of knowing how much there is or how much you'll receive, then you are best to stand back." He nodded to Myra. She smiled at him. "You're a good man, Nolan Bentley. Your father would be most proud of you for what you've done. But you should tell your mother. She should know as well."

Nolan felt his body tense up. "I don't know what you're taking about. And I want you to stay out of my business."

"As you wish. But she should know."

Nolan said nothing as the woman moved away. Glancing around the room, he wondered if anyone else had heard her words, and decided that they were much too busy trying to ignore what was about to happen. He looked at Myra as she seemed to float around the room rather than just walk.

Today the woman was dressed in orange. But it wasn't just the color orange that had him turning away when she moved, but the big black dots that were all over her dress and hair. He wondered if she had her outfits made for her or if she, like most things, made them magically. Whichever it was, there were times that he was glad that he didn't live here anymore. Seeing her as seldom as he did, Nolan had a feeling that her costumes got stranger and stranger daily. He made his way to the deck to get some fresh air.

Nolan had no idea how or why Myra would bring up what he'd been doing lately. It wasn't like he was harming anyone for what he was doing. And he certainly never meant for them to find out. It was his…project, he supposed he could call it, and it made him feel good just knowing that it was his.

The shelter was already there when he hit upon the idea that the homeless, like the ones that worked for Reggie, needed health care. There was a clinic downtown that served a great many people, but where his shelter was, there was a higher population of them. He'd only had to go to the city hall offices and inquire about buying the building next to it, and had ended up with the entire block. Nineteen buildings and a warehouse that was still fully stocked with something. That had been a huge surprise as well.

The warehouse had been a surplus for a now-debunked mattress and bedding store. There were nearly six hundred mattress and box spring sets, over a hundred beds in varying sizes, including cribs and bunk beds, as well as dressers, rocking chairs, and even a few dinette sets. And just the other day they'd unearthed enough towels and sheets to supply even the largest of department stores. They were still sorting through those even as the builders were dividing the place up into small rooms.

The building that he'd planned to buy in the first place was opening their doors in nine days. He had a list of doctors that were coming in to help out, and a list of others that would like to be called should they be needed. And not just general practitioners, but obstetrical-gynecological doctors, optometrists, and two dentists. He'd been able to get enough supplies and equipment to have an x-ray room, a small surgery should it be needed, as well as a birthing suite. And Nolan was broke.

"I think they're ready for you." Nolan turned to look at Reggie when she came out to get him. "Are you all right? You know that if anyone should be nervous, it's me, but I'm surprisingly calm."

"You're never calm, honey. I know that." She grinned when he did. "But I'm not so much nervous as I am uninformed. I know that I should have come to the meeting, but I just couldn't get away. Things needed my attention."

"You're a wonderful doctor, Nolan. You and Burke both are the very best. Joey is going to be happy with his new job and the horses, not to mention him and Chris. Tony has his own practice as well and is doing very well for himself. Garth can make millions out of nothing, and he has for all of us. And we all understand that duty comes first." He didn't tell her it wasn't work but the warehouse, but she hugged him. "Burke just showed up. He is going to be with you. I think Micah will be fine, but you have no idea how glad I am to have you all here."

"We're family, you know." Reggie nodded, and they moved into the house. His mom and grandma were in the kitchen, and he hugged them both before his grandmother asked to speak to him. Nolan told her that she was his forever.

"Behave yourself, young man." He grinned at her, and he could see how hard she was fighting not to laugh with him. "I've some friends in the most odd places."

"Because you're married to Grandda. He has oddities coming out of the woodwork. So when you say that, you're going to have to be a little more specific." She nodded and asked him to have a seat. "I think they're ready for me to help out with Micah."

"They can wait five more minutes. He's had this thing in him for over two months, and a few minutes now won't matter a hill of beans." Nolan sat down. "This friend I was talking about is mine, not Howie's. But he does have a strange group of them. She works as a nurse for Doctor Barlow."

Nolan wanted to try and play it off as he had no idea what she was talking about, but he couldn't lie to her any more than he could his own mom. When he got up to put the tea kettle on the stove, she just watched him.

"You haven't said anything to anyone, have you?" She told him she had not. "I would be really happy if you didn't. It's not something that I want...I know this sounds really crass, but this is my project for now, and I'd like to see if I can do it without their coming in to save me."

"You need saving, Nolan. I know that." He nodded. "How much do you have in the bank? You can't have much."

"I don't. In fact, I might not be able to swing my next rent payment. It's why...after this is over, I'm going to see if I can move in with Mom for a few months. Just to get back on my feet." He turned to her. "It's well worth being broke over. When we open in a few days, there will be so much that can help these people. And Barlow is just the tip of the iceberg in the amount of help I have coming in."

"I'm sure you're going to be a great success, but if the rest of them find out—not from me, but you know that they will—they're not going to be happy to find out you didn't ask for help." He knew that and told her. "Also, here. I want you to have this."

He didn't have to open the envelope to know that it had a check in it. And when he tried to return it to her, she told him to not be silly.

"I can't...I don't know when I can pay you back." For an answer she kissed him on the cheek and walked away from him. It wasn't until then that he looked. It was for a hundred thousand dollars. And Nolan stood in the kitchen and sobbed like a small child at what this meant to him. He'd not even asked, and she had just helped him. Nolan had the best family in the entire world, bar none.

When he thought he could go and see them without them teasing him, Nolan moved into the living room. He kissed his grandmother on the cheek and then went to stand by Micah. He was nervous as hell, and he thought everyone in the room knew it. When Myra asked him to lie on the floor, Micah hugged each and every one of them hard and told him that he loved them.

"You're going to be fine, young man. Just fine." Myra winked at him, then looked at Chris as she continued. "Come now. Let us get this over with. There is things brewing here that must be taken care of soon."

As soon as Micah was laying on the floor of the dining room, both Myra and Chris began to encircle him in a white line of sugar. When Burke asked why sugar, Myra laughed.

"Haven't you heard that you draw more with sweetness than you do with bitterness? It's true of magic as well. Salt is good for bringing someone to you that you want to keep safe or in some cases, hold them, but sugar will be better for what we must do to young Micah here." Grandda asked her why she kept calling him that, young. "Because to me, you all are young. Would you be surprised to know that I have been around for centuries? Not just centuries, but millennia? I know a thing or two about magic."

"Will we live that long too?" Myra only smiled at Chris. "That's not an answer. Will we? I'd really like to know."

"If we do not do this now, I'm afraid that we will have to wait a while longer. I wasn't kidding when I said that things are brewing. Jackson has made contact with a warlock. And if it's all the same to you, I think you'd do better with fighting them both if you had your sister's magic, don't you?" Chris nodded and Nolan thought it was a good idea too. Living long or not at all? It wasn't really a question in his mind. "Now then. Let us begin."

~~~

Joey watched them. He'd been warned, as the rest of them had, not to touch each other during the ceremony. Myra was only going to assist Chris in this, not do it for her. She mentioned that someday she might need to do it again, and it would do her well to know how to do it on her own.

Micah was clad only in his boxers. He had been warned that he should be naked, but he told Myra that it wasn't going to happen. Then she laughed. Joey had a feeling that not only did he not have to be naked, but he could have been bundled in a thick suit of wool with blankets all over him and it wouldn't have made a difference. Still, it was fun to see Micah so nervous.

He'd helped them move the dining room furniture out that morning, and had also helped with gathering the things that Chris would need. He had it in his head that they'd be given a list of things like eye of newt and some dried herbs they'd have to travel to some foreign country for. But it had only been things like heather and sage, as well as a root that grew in the back yard. Myra had said that as a white witch, as Chris was, she could use things that were natural to her. And this was all where they could get it.

The herbs, several bundles of them, were laid on his chest. Myra explained to them what it was to do. Nolan wanted to take notes and even to record what was happening, but he knew that no one would believe him, so all he did was listen.

"The herbs will keep him calm. The heather is made to keep him in a state of rest, the sage will allow him to answer us without pain, should there be any. But there shouldn't be. Chris will do fine."

Chris stood in the circle, then sat on her knees next to Micah. Her dress was as white as the sugar that surrounded them both. She asked Micah if he was ready.

"Yes. I trust you." Chris nodded at Joey's brother and then when he winked, she laughed. "You're going to do this right, Chris. I'm not worried."

"I'm glad one of us isn't." He took her hand and brought it to his mouth for a quick kiss on the back of it. Joey was surprised when his cat purred like it was all right with him. He looked at Reggie and could see that she was fine as well.

The daggers that were laid across Micah's chest were beautiful. He'd gotten to look at them earlier when Myra had brought them to Chris. Each one of them had a different purpose, and Chris was going to have to use them now. When she looked at him, he nodded. All of a sudden, he knew that everything was going to be just fine.

Chris picked up the first of five blades.

"For this I take from you a sample of your flesh to bring Angel McKenzie to me whole." Taking a deep breath, Chris used the knife to slice a small tip off Micah's finger. Taking the small slither of skin to her heart, she then laid it on the smallish wooden table that was beside her. Picking up the next blade, she looked at Micah and at his nod, took it to his hair. "For this I will take from you a part of your being, your cat and you."

The hair, very little of it, was lain next to the skin. The next two blades and samples that she took from Micah were nothing much more than a piece of his fingernail and a drop of his saliva from his mouth. At her look at him again, Joey told her to finish it. Picking up the last of the knives, she told him that she loved him.

"With this blade, enhanced with the blood of my ancestors and magic from their hearts, I take from you, Micah Bentley, holder of my sister's magic, a part of you that no other's seen. I take from you the blood of your heart." When she took Micah's hand in hers and laid it over her thigh, she closed her eyes for only a second before she plunged the knife through his palm. The knife, Joey knew, not only cut through his brother's hand but into her thigh as well.

"Hello sister." Joey, like the rest of them, took a step back from the circle when the woman appeared above Micah's still body. It took Joey a second to realize that she wasn't actually talking to Chris, but this was instead a memory of what had happened the day she died. "I'm sorry about everything. You have no idea how much...I wish I had more time. I'm saving this man, who gave his life for not just me but for you as well. I want you to have this and no other. You are the stronger of the two of us anyway. Go to the building where we were queens and you'll find the rest that I have given you. Tell Dad...tell Dad that I loved him more than I ever did my own father, and that I will miss him as much as I do you."

Joey watched through Angel's viewpoint what happened that day. Micah was there as well, his body covered in blood, and the wound in his back, they could see now, had been fatal. Angel healed him at a great cost to herself by pushing her magic into him. The wounds sealed and he breathed again. When his body disappeared, so did the vision. But this was far from finished.

Joey started to reach for Chris, and the second that he did, Nolan touched him. To more than likely warn him, he was sure, but his connection to him made them both become a part of the storm that seemed to come out of nowhere in the circle. As they were sucked in, Joey felt as if he were being sucked through a straw, but held onto Nolan when his hand suddenly appeared in front of his face.

Images of his life, of his brothers, and then of Chris and Angel slammed into his head. Memories of things that happened to them all as children, as adults, then in the future seemed to blend together, merge into one loop of a movie.

Joey saw children that were born to him. His brother being hurt by a gunshot one day, and the wife that would make his brother so happy that he was forever smiling. His mother happy, having a child on each arm as she took them to the swing set that had yet to be built. Grandda sitting in a chair at the end of a dock, fishing and talking to a small boy. Grandma working in a garden, her flowers as bright as the smile on her face as a little girl stood beside her helping. He saw Micah and Reggie with a houseful of children, all of them sitting around a large Christmas tree and happy. As the storm began to calm, the force of it seeming to lessen, he saw other things, things that made his heart ache in pain.

The long procession of a funeral, the black limo holding him and the others. Flowers surrounding an open grave, his mom and grandmother quietly crying under a canopy. Grandda, his heart said, and he felt the pain more in the knowing that he'd die. As the images slowed more, he saw things that were more now, in this time, and saw a man on the lawn with his family. He wasn't Jackson Hill, but a man that he'd never known. And he was powerful.

This time when the people moved, the places changed, he saw Nolan standing in front of a building, lines of the homeless and sick going into it. He stood back, Nolan did, and watched. In this he wore nothing more than a tattered coat, his pockets turned out as if to show that there was nothing in them. Joey settled down. His feet seemingly touched the ground as he looked at Nolan. He was sad, his heart heavy. Joey turned back to the building and nearly wept with what he saw.

"I named it for Dad." Joey nodded. "But it took all I had. I should have asked for your help. For all of your help, and now it will close."

"No it won't." Joey looked at Nolan, and his face changed. Burke was there and he was crying. "What is it?"

"I'm not happy." Joey asked him why. "Because I'm a failure. I'm simply a failure. And I've no reason to live."

The pain in his head had the dreams or whatever they were fade out. The next pain, sharper than the last, seemed to bring him around. Joey opened his eyes and looked at Burke, who was standing over him, his hand drawn back to hit him again. Joey told him he was awake. That he was all right.

"What the fuck were you thinking? Huh? What were you told several times to do before this ever began?" Joey never got a chance to answer because Burke seemed to be on a roll then. "You were told not to touch anyone until this was finished. Until Myra—who I might add is in the kitchen with your wife—until she told you to. But you had to do it. You and Nolan just had to do what you were told not to, just like when we were kids."

"You're not happy, why?" Burke drew back as if he'd hit him too. "You're not a failure, you know. You're the best doctor I know, and the hospital is very lucky to have you on staff."

"Who...what are you talking about?" Joey was helped up off the floor, but his brother and then he looked around before speaking again. "I'm not even going to justify what you're talking about with anything. You're nuts."

"But you're not a failure, Burke. If you want out of what you do, then stop it, but I think you're doing a great job. And no matter what, I'm so proud to call you brother." Burke looked away, then back at him. "I love you."

"I can't save them." Joey nodded. "I try, but sometimes it's just not enough. I can't...I know I can't save them all, but it's getting harder and harder to even save a few."

"Burke, do you like what you're doing? Even if it's only the few, do you still like it?" Burke didn't answer him but just looked at the picture of their dad that hung over the fireplace. "You think he would have wanted you to be unhappy in what you're doing? What would he say to you right now, you think?"

"He'd say to me, boy, what are you whining about? Get in there and have some dinner with your family and buck up." Joey didn't say anything but waited on Burke. "He'd tell me to be proud of what I'm doing and if I can't, find something that does make me proud."

"He'd say that."

Burke looked at him then. "Nolan has been asking me to go into practice with him. I think...I'm going to do it. The emergency room is just...I need a connection with the people I help. I don't get that with working there. Nolan said that he has patients, whole families, that come to see him, and he gets to see them from birth to death. I think...I really think that's what I need."

Joey had no idea if Burke would be any happier there or in the hospital, but change, he'd discovered, was good. As they made their way into the kitchen, a gathering place in any of their homes, he'd discovered, he asked Nolan how he was.

"You know that wasn't real, right? I'm not a hobo." His voice was hard, like he was pissed off about what Joey might have seen. "I want you to stay out of my personal life, Joey. All of you. I'm doing just fine."

Joey decided that because of what he wasn't saying rather than what he'd just said to him, Joey was going to have a look into his brother's life. It wasn't prying, he told himself, but making sure. Something had happened to Nolan, and he wanted to find out before things got too far. Or if they were already too far. They were family, after all.

Chapter 12

"What is it?" Chris watched as the big crane-like thing attached to the back of the semi unloaded the large crate. It had arrived yesterday while they'd been at Micah's house, and they were just now getting around to opening it. "Did he leave you a note? Any clue?"

"No. Just this." He handed her the note which simply said: *Open with someone you love.* "What do you suppose it is? And why does it need to be guarded until we open it?"

"I have no clue. I've had enough crap going on lately that I just don't know what is right or wrong anymore." Joey just grinned at her and pulled her to his body. "I have to admit that I'm glad it went well. I was terrified."

The letting, as it was called, that she'd done to Micah had left her feeling no different. Her sigil, like Joey's, was now up and over her shoulder and down her back. And instead of on her hand, as it had been, it now was from her elbow to her shoulder.

"I knew you could do it. You're my mate, after all." The guard that seemed to be in charge cleared his throat, and both Joey and she turned to him. He has been so close to them since they'd come out of the house that she was beginning to think that he was going to come with the box too.

"Mr. Bentley, if you'll just tell us where you want it, we'll make sure it gets there." Joey asked the man what part of the house it went in. "Wherever you want. We took it out of the warehouse the moment we were told that Mr. Emmett passed away. It's been...no one has been near this since we started keeping an eye on it for him."

"How long is that?" The man looked down at his paper and told him the date. Joey looked at her, and she could see that it meant something to him. "That's the day that I interviewed for the job at Peck and Simmons. Surely you have that wrong."

"No sir. We were hired to not just keep an eye on it, but every year on that date Mr. Peck came to see us and put something in it. I don't know what, but he was very clear that we were to take it to you the day he was pronounced deceased." Joey nodded and asked if they could please take in into the barn.

"If it's something to go into the house, then I guess we can have it moved there later. But I want to open this so that's as good a place as any." The men, twelve of them, helped to tie the straps to the carte and the mover took it to the barn.

Chris watched them and as soon as it was set down, she moved to it and put her hand on it. She had no idea why, but she knew that if she touched it, it would tell her what was inside. As soon as her fingers touched the wood, she turned to Joey and smiled.

"You're not going to believe this. But there is a witch's curse on this. Myra's handiwork, I think." She couldn't tell what was in it, but she knew that they really did have to open it with the family around them. She knew that it would benefit them all. That whatever was inside was for them all to see.

It took the men nearly five hours to get the thing off the truck and into the barn. Chris invited the men to dinner and went to tell Carol that they'd be joining them, and the woman started taking potatoes out of the big oven. There were five loaves of bread, still steaming on the counter, as well as a large salad and the biggest pile of bacon she'd ever seen. Carol informed her that the steaks would be done when they were ready and not a minute before. Chris started to ask her if she wanted to know how they wanted them cooked and thought she'd already know that. Instead, Chris answered the phone when it rang.

"I've decided to take you up on your offer to come out and see you." It took Chris a few seconds to think who was talking when it occurred to her that it was Jackson. "I need to clear up a few things with you, and I'd like to get them over with before I have to go and find me a job."

He was lying to her, as only another witch would be able to do, but he did not lie very well. She had no idea how she knew that or why it mattered, but she reached across the phone lines and into his head. She saw the man he'd been talking to, as well as the plan for him to come to their home. Chris felt calmed by the news. It would soon be over with and she could move on with her life. When she turned to write down some notes of the things she'd seen there, Myra was making herself a cup of tea with Carol, and the two of them watched her.

"Invite him here. Tomorrow should be good, don't you think, sister?" Carol nodded at Myra. "That would be a wonderful time, and we'll have time to prepare you both for his visit."

Jackson saying her name again had Chris going back to the phone conversation. "Tomorrow is the best I can do, Jackson. I can send you a car then, around...." Myra held up three fingers. "Three o'clock good with you?"

"Yes, yes. That's fine. I'll expect you to be on time too. And if you're going to make me wait all day, you should at least have me in for dinner."

Something about that made her sigil move along her skin, and Chris decided that no matter what, he wasn't coming into her home.

"I'll make sure that he's on time. I'll see you tomorrow then." While he was still talking, Chris hung up the phone. Looking at the two women, she asked them to please have a seat. "Now. Tell me why I feel like him coming here is a bad idea. And why he's so not coming into my house."

Carol turned and looked at Myra, though how she looked at her for very long was a mystery to her. The woman was in the brightest shade of purple that she'd ever seen. It seemed to just glow with color.

"Didn't I tell you she was smart? I told you just yesterday morning that this grand witch is the smartest of them all." Myra said that she had said it. "And here she is just brimming with knowledge that no one gave her, save the man on the phone. Which warlock do you suppose is coming here with—?"

"Whoa there, ladies." They both turned to look at her. "Who is...what grand witch are you talking about? And what do you mean, a warlock is coming? I don't want either of them here. I have enough shit going on without that too."

"Why, darling, you're the grand witch, and that makes...well, I guess I never thought of it until just this second, but your husband is your warlock. Oh my, and your familiar too. A cat and a witch. Isn't that just grand? What a pair you two are. And oh my, your children are going to be just simply the strongest beings ever born." Chris sat down hard as Carol continued. The two of them were speaking, but for the life of her, Chris had no idea what they were saying. Then the door to the kitchen burst open and there was Joey's cat.

"Joey?"

The big black cat snarled and stared at the two women. Chris had no idea what had happened to make him come in like that, but her own cat was clawing at her to come out as well. When Joey spoke to her, she nearly laughed, but she wasn't sure it would be something he'd appreciate.

I felt your fear. And I have to tell you, I've never been on the receiving end of something so powerful in my life. I think…are you all right? She told him she was just fine. *Then would you mind telling me what the fuck is going on? My cat wants blood.*

"I'm the grand witch." Joey sat down on his haunches, and she felt her cat purr then. "They just told me that since you're a cat, you're both my familiar and my warlock. Do you know what that means?"

The cat part or the familiar part? She told him both. *The cat part is me. Why would I need that explained to me?*

"You're a panther, but that's not what I mean. And I'm not saying I believe them, but as my familiar, I can use you. You can be my eyes when I need you to be. And you can help me when I have a spell, if I were to believe all the folklore."

He said that he still didn't understand, and Chris turned to Myra to ask her to explain.

"You're her familiar, darling. The thing that not just holds her magic for her, but you enhance it. When you're beside her as a cat, her magic and yours is doubly strong, and…well, it's more controlled too. Like you're her vault." Myra stood up, her body tense and alert. Joey stood as well with his fur standing on end along his back. Even his teeth seemed to have gotten bigger. "Tyron is coming."

~~~

Tyron moved around his hotel room waiting for the fool to call him. Jackson Hill was as useless as he'd thought he'd be, and if he hadn't needed him to get into the house, he would have killed him. But to get to the grand witch, he had to use him, if only for a little while longer.

As he walked the room, all this hope for this to work depending on Jackson, he thought of the woman. Chris McKenzie was going to be his ticket to a brighter and easier lifestyle. Not just with her magic, but everything that came with being married to the grand witch as well. And marry him she would. Or if it came to it, he'd have to kill her. Which wasn't out of the question right now.

He'd heard the stories about the girls. Not their names, of course, but that they were out there. And he had searched for years for even a glimpse of what they might look like. Not that looks mattered, and he'd never seen Chris. But if Chris looked anything, even a little bit, like her sister, then she was going to be a beauty. But it was their hidden talent that had him trying to find them.

Their mother, a witch of the highest order anyway, had left the coven she'd been in to raise her daughters. Her husband was a warlock that had taken Deb as his wife, even against her will when he'd found out what she'd been. It was only a short year later that Angel had been born, and a year after that, Chris. They all heard about it. The warlock could talk of nothing else but his very well marked daughters. But after his death, they all seemed to fall off the edge of the earth.

Then about five years ago, he'd heard that Angel was making the rounds with her magic. And it had been a powerful push into not just the coven that he had belonged to but rarely frequented, but the magical world as well. He'd kept an eye on her, not very closely as it turned out, but he'd known about where she was at all times and hoped that the other sister would turn up too. But she hadn't. Then about a year ago, he'd heard that she'd let her magic go and that even when pushed, Chris never used it. He had written her off, much as he had her mother.

The magical world had taken a blow when it was announced that Angel had been killed. And by one of their own. Jackson Hill, even indirectly, had murdered her and had lost his chance to get her magic. Tyron had gone to the place where she'd been killed and could see nothing that would make him believe that she'd been anything more than a level one or maybe two witch. Until Myra came to the coven to make an announcement.

"Jackson Hill is no longer allowed to be a part of this or any coven. He has killed the sister to the grand witch." There were murmurs around the room so loud that Tyron stood up to tell them to be silent. The sound of his voice had the room as still as a church. "As I was saying, the grand witch has made herself known to me. And once she is reunited with her sister's magic, she will come to us as our leader. Jackson Hill will be killed on sight, as well as anyone helping him from now on."

Tyron had made it his business to look into this Hill person, then the sister of Angel. He'd nearly made a mistake in writing her off until he saw her with her mate three days ago. She was most assuredly the grand witch, and her magic was stronger than his would ever be. Unless he was married to her. And that was his plan.

He didn't care if she was married now or not. When Tyron wanted something, he made it so that it was his. Killing was as easy to him as breathing. And he'd done it so much in the name of his magic that he knew that it was just as much a part of his makeup as putting on his shoes or pants. It was his, no matter who or what was in the way when he went to get it. A panther would be just as easy to kill as a human.

Tyron had made it his business to find out as much as he could about the Bentleys. He knew that the oldest, Micah, had been recently wed and that he and his wife had two daughters. The fact that he had adopted something as inferior to him as human children made Tyron realize that they were all fools. And Joseph Bentley wasn't much different.

Who bought land and raised horses that were better off dead? No one that he knew. The fact that they were brought to him instead of the slaughter house made Tyron think that the man had a soft heart. And a soft heart also meant a soft head. He had to have one if he was doing something as idiotic as what he was attempting to do now. So taking his wife was going to be a piece of cake. And the fact that Chris had no real knowledge of her talent, if everything he'd heard about her was true, meant she'd be easy as well.

When his phone rang, Tyron let it ring three times before he went to answer it. The hotel had been warned not to let any calls through but those from Jackson.

"Did you really think that I'd not override your rules, Tyron? I mean, really. I've been around long enough—longer than you—that I have picked up a few tricks of my own." He sat down on the edge of the bed and slid to the floor. "You do know who this is, don't you? Your good friend, Myra."

"You're not my friend." Her laughter made him think of nails down a chalkboard. "What the hell could you possibly want?"

"This and that. You should know that I've had a close eye on the grand witch. She's more powerful than you can imagine. And that mate of hers, did you know that he's her familiar as well?" He hadn't, but he should have thought of that. Bentleys were cats. "The man is positively oozing with power. You should...oh, I was going to say you should see them, but you're going to, aren't you?"

"What are you talking about?" Tyron was going to kill Jackson. He had told them what he'd wanted and now it was going to blow up in his face. "I have no idea what you're talking about."

"Such a terrible liar. And she won't allow you in the house. I didn't have to tell her that either. But she saw it. When she was talking to your flunky. Is that what they call them now? The ones that are used for their own purposes?" Her laughter again. "I think there's a rule about that somewhere. I'll have to look it up. Personal gain is something they teach you in the first year, I believe. Or have you thought of yourself as above such things?"

Her voice had grown hard and cold at the end. She was mad, and a mad Myra was a very scary witch. When she appeared in front of him, Tyron put the phone down and stared at her. He wondered if he could kill her, but decided that she just wasn't worth messing with right now. He had bigger fish to kill.

"What is it you want? To warn me off as you did the other witch? It won't work. I'm not one of those little people you like to order around. I'm well within my rights to do what I need to do to take her." She moved around the room slowly. He was grateful for that. Her outfit today was one that could make you deathly ill should she move too quickly. The purple was a shade that he was sure that she'd made herself, and the pink and green paisley that was the pattern was too much. Even her hair was sporting the same colors.

"I'm not here to warn you about anything. What a thing to say to me. But I will tell you that you're not going to win with this one. She's...she's more powerful than I've ever seen." He could tell that she really believed that, and he got a slight chill from the way she seemed to be in awe of the girl. "When you come—because I've no doubt that you will—know that the council will be there as well. There will be no wrongdoing on either of your parts. We'll make sure of that. Oh, and you might want to rethink taking her mate. While I think it would be hilarious to see you try, you're just going to piss them off, and that will make things end too quickly for me. I need a good show now and again."

"You think they can take me? Or is it you think they can kill me?" She didn't answer but sat on the edge of his bed. "You do know who you're talking to, right? I'm a warlock, not some witch that has nothing better to do than to believe your bullshit."

"Do you know the definition to the word warlock, Tyron?" He nodded. All knew what the word meant. Few had ever really considered it, but he knew just what he was. "The dictionary says simply that a warlock is a man that practices the black arts. That's not true by the way. Most do, but I know one or two that don't. It also says that they're a sorcerer or a conjurer. But there are other places that you can find a more...I want to say meaningful definition. It states that one has a demonic power. That they only see...opportunity. An opportunity, I think, you'll agree that serves them and only them. They dominate over imps of the underworld. Yet, you have none. Not any more, do you?"

Tyron hated this woman and her abundance of knowledge that was not hers to have. "There are rules everywhere that you're expected to follow. Most of them are idiotic or even useless. He thought…it matters little what he thought when they were summoned back from me. But I will lead an army one day soon, and when I do, you'll bow before me."

"You think so." He didn't answer her and wasn't even sure that he could have. The power that seemed to surround him took his breath away. "I could end your very existence right now. Take your power and keep it as my own. You'd be nothing, not even a footnote in the world of magic."

He was struggling to breathe now. Even his attempts to raise his magic weren't working. She stood over him now, her face close enough that he could see right into her very soul. And for the first time in a very long time, Tyron felt horrific fear, the death of everything that he was and knew. And he also knew that Myra would not be the one to take it.

When she disappeared, Tyron sucked in as much air as his lungs would allow, and it still wasn't enough. Laying on the cool carpet, he tried to control his breathing enough that he no longer felt the urge to pass out, and his heart began to beat at a normal pace. The laughter, Myra's again, flooded his head, and when he sat up, he realized that he was light-headed and dizzy. The phone ringing had him nearly jump up off the floor.

When it rang the second time, he picked it up. The voice at the other end sounded like Jackson, but he wasn't sure anymore.

"Tyron? Are you all right? I have the times that I'm going to the house. You there?"

"I'm here." Jackson told him that he had been worried. "You should worry about yourself. I'm perfectly fine. What time do you get out there?"

"She's sending me a car. Nice, right? It's the least she could do, after what she put me through. The fucking cunt. Did I tell you what Myra and she did to my dinner? I swear to you, when I have Angel's magic, I'm going to tear Myra apart." He told him he didn't care. "Oh, yeah. Well, I'm going to be picked up at three o'clock. She said that they're going to have dinner ready when I arrive. I guess it's going to be easier to get into the house than I thought. I'll just have to go to the bathroom or something. But I'm not eating anything even if they do offer it to me. I'm having a dinner before I go out."

"Just get in the house and call me." Jackson said that he would. "When you get there, I want you to make sure that you say nothing about me coming out. Do you understand me? I don't want them to know that I'm even thinking about coming out there."

"I can do that, but I think she already knows." He asked him who knew. "Chris and her husband. He was the one that called me. Then I talked to Chris. They're expecting you. She said for me to tell you that you're so fucked."

Tyron sat there for a long time. His mind was working over all the details that he'd been planning since he'd found Chris. And even though now he knew that he shouldn't have, he had left out the fact that Myra would be involved. He knew now that in order to get to the magic he wanted, he was going to have to kill Myra. She'd been a pain in his ass for a very long time, and it was very past time to end her reign over them all.

He thought about calling out to the demonic warlock that had helped him before, but also knew that they had not parted on good terms. In fact, their parting had nearly been fatal to him. And the fact that he was told to never summon him again made Tyron a little nervous to do so now. But the demon warlock hated Myra as much as he did. She'd been his biggest failure when it came to killing witches.

"Lord of the underworld, I summon thee." The heat was the first indication that he got that he was in trouble. The second thing was the vision of being moved, and quickly. When Tyron opened his eyes, he looked around. Instead of bringing the demon to him, the demon had brought him to his world. He really was fucked.

Chapter 13

Joey stretched out; his cat needed this more than he'd realized. And as soon as he was tackled from behind, he had to sheath his claws or hurt her. He stood up and looked at Chris when she stood by him.

You're supposed to be resting. He watched her body as she stretched much like he'd done, her head almost down to the ground, her ass in the air. He felt his panther snarl along his skin to take her, but he asked him…begged him…to wait. *I thought we agreed that you'd wait before you shifted. And not to do it alone.*

I wasn't alone. Nolan helped me. Well, he helped me get out of the house. He said to tell you to not leave me to my own devices next time. I think I might have broken a few pieces of the new furniture in my haste to figure out what I was doing. Did you know that when you run in the house like this, you have no balance? He told her that he did know that. It was why they didn't shift in the house. *Your mom said that she'd put us out some lunch. And for us not to hurry. You think this will take very long? She thought perhaps you could show me a few tricks.*

His befuddled mind could only focus on one thing at a time, and right now it was working on keeping his mind off of running her down and fucking her. When she moved to him, she rubbed her body alongside of his. Joey nipped at her shoulder when she passed him.

Do you have any idea what you're doing to me? Chris laughed in his mind, and he watched her move. *You're beautiful as a cat. Did Nolan mention that to you?*

No. All he did was laugh, then tell me what I already told you. Are you going to run me down, Joey? You've been telling me you want to for days now. She stretched again. *My cat is very needy. And so am I. It's like she wants you, but doesn't. But I do.*

How do you want me, Chris? Do you want me to fuck you like this? Or did you have something else in mind?

When she tensed up, so did he. Neither of them moved when the large deer came out of the tree line and stared at them. As soon as he took off in the opposite direction, Joey returned to his mate.

I want you to run me down. I want you to chase me, catch me, and take me like this. Then I want you to shift to yourself so that I can lick your cock until you are so ready to come that once I shift, as soon as you enter me, we both come. He growled low at her, and she moved back. *Would you, Joey?*

Yes. He backed from her. The need to take her right here was making his cat angry. He wanted her as his wife too, as a woman. But he only stood up and told her one word, and it was enough. *Run.*

Joey knew where she was at all times. She was noisy, first of all, and secondly, her scent was on everything that she touched. He reached out to her when he saw her fall over a downed log and asked her if she was all right.

Yes. But why can't I hear you? I mean, this is great that I can hear everything, but not you. I want to do this right so I can hide from you. Joey moved out from behind the tree, and she watched his steps as he moved. He was careful not to break a branch or crush too many leaves as he moved. *How do you know where to step if you're watching me?*

Listen as you put your foot down. If you hear the slightest bit of noise, I can hear it too. Your paw is very sensitive as well. You can feel branches before you touch them. Smell the area around you. You can tell the difference between the dry grasses and the marsh. Step in the wet areas carefully as well. There might be an animal there that you disturb, and I'll hear that too. She moved then. While she wasn't silent like him, she was a good deal quieter. *That's it. Now when you move by something, don't let it brush up against you. Go lower than it if you need, leap over it if you have to. Your scent is all over the forest now because your fur marked it.*

It was coming to her slowly, but she was working hard at it. Once she came upon a branch that she'd broken, he watched her sniff it and back away. He asked her what she smelled.

Man. He nodded. He'd smelled it too when he'd first come out here, and knew that it was his grandda. Just the other day he'd told him that someone was on their land. Joey told him to warn the others. *It's not anyone I know, is it?*

I thought it was Grandda. But there is someone here that we have to watch out for. Can you tell me if it's a shifter or not? She sniffed again and turned to look at him. *What do you smell?*

Aftershave. Men's. And something flowery like…I think its fabric softener. He told her it was. *There is something else. A chemical that I know but can't think what it might be right now.*

You want me to tell you?

She shook her head no and took off running. It was smoother now…her steps were more precise and her leaps were controlled. He could hear her, but not like before. Joey gave her a head start before he moved to capture her once more.

She was always close to him. But he did miss her a couple of times when she doubled back on him. Chris was learning fast; her scent was weaker now that she wasn't touching everything, and he was thrilled when he was tackled again by her. This time she stayed near him instead of taking off again.

Joey let her mark him. Her body moved along his back and forth until his own cat wanted her marked as well. As he moved up behind her, Chris asked him if it would hurt this way.

No. I mean, I don't think so. But you're not going to enjoy it. I have no idea why, but I've heard that cats, the female anyway, rarely enjoy being mounted by their mates. When he moved over her, her cat snarled at him. *She knows that she's being dominated and doesn't care for it. But I can't wait any longer.*

Her cat fought him but not too much. Joey knew that he wanted her as much as he did Chris, but this was something that the cat in him needed too. To mark her cat. When she tried to move from under him, Joey begged her to be still.

He'll bite you.

She reared up and nearly knocked him off her, but Joey knew that his cat was stronger. As he bit into her shoulder, he heard Chris scream out in pain. So did her cat.

It was a quick coupling. He mounted her, fucked her hard, then came. He supposed his cat was much like most teenaged boys in that respect. Love them and leave them. But when Chris's cat moved and snarled at him, he shifted into his body and stood very still.

She wants to bite you. And to taste you. Nodding, Joey fisted his cock. He was a little afraid of her...she was a panther first and foremost. *Can I taste you like this?*

172

"Yes. But I'm going to eat you when your cat has had her fill." Telling him she was looking forward to it, she moved closer to him. "Don't bite my cock. I think that would be the worst kind of pain."

She won't. Her tongue lapped along his length, and Joey moaned. Christ, he'd never had anyone do that to him before, and wondered why he'd waited. Then he watched Chris and knew the answer. He'd been waiting for her. *I can taste me on you...my cat, I mean, and your precum. You taste delicious to us both. Move your hands and don't touch us.*

He did as she asked and wrapped his hands around the branch above his head. Her tongue wrapped around his cock over and over until he thought for sure he was going to die from the pleasure. But when she moved to his balls, he tensed up until she licked him there. Joey begged her to do it again.

He was hurting now. His balls and cock were so full that he knew that if she told him to come or even touched him again, he was going to lose it. Instead of bringing him, which he wanted in the worst kind of way, Chris shifted to her body.

Joey grabbed her and picked her up. She was thankfully wet enough that when he pulled her down over his cock, he slid home. Turning her so that her back was to the tree, Joey fucked her as hard as he could while she held onto his shoulders, her legs wrapped around his waist.

"Bite me when you come." Her nod wasn't enough for him. "Say it, tell me you're going to bite me when you come."

"I'm going to tear into your flesh and drink from you as soon as you fill me."

Joey cried out, her words fueling him in ways that he'd never felt before. As he emptied into her, filling her as she'd

173

commanded, he tilted his head and let her have his throat. She did indeed tear into him, and he did the same to her shoulder when he came a second, then a third time.

Holding her was all he could manage. If someone had come up to them, Joey could no more protect them than he could beg them to stay back. Every part of him was empty. Had he not been leaning against the tree, he was sure that he would have fallen over.

Her giggle had him lifting his head about an inch. That was all he had in him.

"I can see why your mom thought we'd be out here a while. Do you suppose she knew we were going to have sex?" Joey didn't answer. His mom knew everything, and he'd not be surprised to learn that she'd sent Chris out here just for that reason. "I really love her, by the way. Your grandparents too."

"Good, but if it's all the same to you, I'd just as soon not talk about my mom or my grandparents when I'm buried inside of you buck naked." Her laughter had him smiling. "Christ, you nearly killed me. Your cat must have been really needy."

"She was." When Chris shifted her body against his, he wondered if she was hurting. The tree was rough, and he was sure that he'd pounded her pretty hard against it. "I need to put my legs down. And I think…I kinda hurt on my ass."

He let her down but held onto her, mostly to keep himself upright but to steady her as well. His knees felt as if they were made completely of rubber right now. When he felt sturdier, he tried to remember where he'd left his clothing. When Chris said his name softly, he turned to look at her.

She was pointing to the pack of wolves that was standing near the lake. Not moving too fast, he stood in front of her and tried to cover himself as best he could. The pack, all wolves but some of them shifters, he noticed, were all looking down at the ground except the one in the middle.

We were sent here by Emmett. He said to protect you at all costs. Joey asked him how long he'd been there. *Not long. We didn't witness your coupling, but we...we protected you.*

"Did I need protecting?" The wolf looked in the direction of the lake again and Joey saw them then. There were two men there, both of them with guns, and each carrying a dead rabbit. "How long have you been tracking them?"

Two days. We have been keeping an eye on them so that they don't hunt on your land, but the property over there, across the lake, isn't yours. I might suggest you purchase it. He would if he could. *There is something else you should know. The thing in the barn, you should open it soon. It will...help me.*

"Help you?" The wolf laid down and just stared at him. "I've been...we have a problem coming our way, and we wanted to deal with that before looking into what Emmett has left us."

Open it as soon as you can. I need for you to as much as the other wolves do. Joey told him he would. *Your clothing is behind you. And that of the female. She is a witch, isn't she?*

Joey looked at Chris, then at the wolf again. "She is a witch. That's what we're having the issue about." The wolf nodded and looked at the wolves on the end. When they took off in the direction of the men, Joey asked him what was going on.

We're going to frighten them a bit more. The last time they were here, they shot one of the deer on this side and left it to die on its own. I know that hunting is a sport, but it only bothers me when they kill one of my own or leave behind what they don't want. And before you ask, I'm not going to harm them. Not this time anyway.

Joey thanked him and turned to look at Chris.

"I know you, don't I?" The wolf said that she did. "The Walton case. It was your child that was killed. I was the lawyer that represented you in the trial. I'm sorry how it went. But I want you to come to the house in the morning. I have something that belongs to you, I think. I'd had it in my office for a few weeks, and when they packed my things up, it was sent here. It belongs to your son."

Justice has been served. Chris nodded but said no more to Mr. Walton. *My name is Drew Walton. I will be around in the morning then.*

As he left them, all the pack followed. Joey wanted to ask her about the case, but could see that she was struggling with something. He held her in his arms once they were both dressed and ready to leave.

"I lost it because of the police. They didn't process the killer right and it came back to bite them in the ass. The guy got off with nothing but time served. Last time I heard, he was suing the state for that time too." She lifted her head and looked at him. "Does he mean that he killed the man?"

"I think so. When he comes tomorrow, I want to talk to him about the box in the barn. I'm worried now that it's been there for so long." He took her hand in his as they headed back to the house.

Just on the edge of the tree line was a basket from his mom. They sat down and ate while they talked about nothing much at all. Then he remembered the last delivery coming to them. "They should be here sometime later in the week. We could take on so many more if we had the means. But things are tight right now, what with me having to take care of Emmett's firm and some of the other things that he left for me to see to."

As they made their way into the house some time later, Joey realized that after tonight things might be normal again. Or as normal as it could get for his family. Grandda was in the kitchen when he went in to see about dinner. He was smiling like a loon, and that worried him more than when Grandda was frowning.

"Boy, I've got a deal for you. Come on in the office with me. Micah and I have something to tell you." Joey asked if he needed Chris and was told she was already there. Joey almost dreaded something else happening. He was exhausted with it all now.

~~~

Everything was set. The table and chairs on the lawn were all arranged, and the food was being brought out even as the limo pulled up in the drive. Joey came to stand next to Chris, and she took his hand like a lifeline. Soon, she kept telling herself, soon this would be over.

"We're not going inside to eat?" Jackson looked a little panicky, and she told him that they decided that it would be more fun to eat out in the nice sunshine. "Well, then…can I use the bathroom?"

"I'm sorry, Jackson, but the bathroom on the main floor isn't finished being renovated. There is the one in the barn you can use. But I'm afraid you'll find it to be a little small. It's used by the men that work for us, and they didn't need a shower." He looked at the barn then the house. "You're welcome to go now if you want."

As he made his way to the barn, she looked at Gracie. The woman had gone well and above the call of duty today. Not only had she gotten all the food organized, but she'd also thought of the bathroom in the barn. When Jackson came out of the barn a few minutes later, he was on his cell phone. Tuning into what he was saying, Chris had to hide a smile. This was great.

"I don't know what you want me to do. Short of running in the house around the several hundred people that seem to be here, I don't know what you want me to do." The phone was jerked from his ear, and Chris would bet that Tyron was screaming at him to fix it. She was glad now that she'd listened to Myra when she explained why he wanted in the house.

"He'd have control of it. Ownership, I guess you could call it. Once he's inside he can call on his power to make the home and the contents his. Including you. Joey would be his too, and it would be easy for him then to have Joey kill himself rather than Tyron dealing with it himself." Chris had asked her why the house and not anything else, say the barn. "Because the house and all that is in it is yours, the two of you. The barn, while it does belong to you both, isn't anything you think of when you treasure things. The barn is just what you'd think it would be, a place to store animals."

"So he'd use our love of where we live against us?" Myra told her that was right. "You could have too. It's why you couldn't come in until I invited you."

"No. That is different. I'm a witch. Tyron is a warlock. I'm bound by the laws of my kind...not to enter a dwelling until you are invited. Tyron being what he is, he's not bound by the same rules. He needs to be summoned into the house by someone inside. And once there, he can do what he pleases to whomever he wants. Because he was summoned, it would be difficult if not impossible to get him out again."

So dinner was being served in the yard and the only bathroom was in the barn. As they sat down, the entire family surrounding her, Jackson was at the end of the table with not just Myra and Carol, but a man that had shown up not ten minutes before Jackson had. Myra said that he was the council president and would be observing the happenings of the day.

Joey passed the potato salad toward the end of the table where Jackson was and cleared his throat. It was ready to begin. "So, Jackson, I'm to understand that you're here to take the magic of my sister-in-law. It won't work, in the event you're wondering. I have it. Well, some of it. Chris has the—"

"It's mine. I was to get it." He stood up and slammed his hands down on the table as he spoke. "You were not allowed to take it. The rules clearly state that I can have it because I'm a stronger witch than she was. Not that I had anything to do with her death, not directly anyway, but I want it returned to me."

"No you weren't. Had you been then you would have killed her yourself, you moron. And how did you propose I give it to you?" Jackson only smiled at Joey. "I'm not going to kill myself over this. And from what I've been told, there was no magic within Angel when you had her killed, so therefore, it belongs to the person she held it for. My brother."

Jackson looked around the table and then back at them. "You will give it to me then. There is a way for you to remove it from him, and then I can have it." Joey was shaking his head. "Why the hell not? I told you, it was not against any law that I took it."

"Are you saying that you had her killed for this magic you believed she had?" Everyone turned to Micah.

179

"Angel…you said that you took it fairly. You mean you had her killed, or you killed her for her magic, and that's how it belongs to you?"

"Yes. You've been studying our laws. Or someone has told you. But yes, she was killed by a magical creature that I hired to take her magic. And someone here has it." Micah told him that she'd given it to him before she'd been killed. "Then you will give it to me."

The magic, the power of it, had Chris standing up. As Jackson waved his fingers in the air, Chris pushed him back, took his power, and shoved it back at him tenfold. His magic hit him in the chest, much like he'd planned for it to hit Micah, only more of it. When he stood up after a minute or two, she could see that he thought Myra had done it when she had.

"You will not harm my family." He looked at her, then raised his hands again. This time she not only pushed him back, but pinned him against the barn wall that was about ten feet from where they were. "And you will not get my sister's magic. Not now, not so long as there is breath in my body."

"I can arrange it so that you are dead, should you like." His smile had her stepping back from him. "I'm not going to fuck around with you and this shit hole any longer."

As he peeled from the wall, she lifted her hands. She wasn't really sure what she could do to stop him, but he wasn't going to hurt her family. When he dropped to his knees, his clothing suddenly gone, she took another step back, then another until she backed into Joey.

"I summon thee, Tyron the Warlock. Come to me."

The air around them seemed to heat up exponentially. When she was sure that her own skin was going to burn from her flesh, a cooling breeze blew over her and she let out her breath slowly. When she saw the man that was there, Tyron no doubt, Chris knew that they were all in deep trouble.

He was what Myra had warned her about. The warlock that had made deals with the underworld. The warlock Tyron, in all his glory and magic.

"Hello, my bride. Are you ready for me?"

Chapter 14

Joey felt his cat. He was almost afraid to shift, but when Myra told him to do it, he let him take his body. In seconds he was standing there with his mate, and when she put her hand on his head, Joey nearly whimpered.

It wasn't painful, not even close to that, but it was powerful. He could feel her magic dancing along his body from hers, and he moved closer to her. Leaning his big body into hers, Joey knew that they could conquer worlds should they need to. But right now, he'd be satisfied with killing this prick that had come uninvited to their home.

"I'm ready for you. But are you sure you want to go there?" The monster snarled at Chris when she laughed at him. "You can't harm me. You should know that by now. Why don't you just leave and we'll forget this ever happened?"

Tyron looked evil; his body wasn't human at all, but he looked like a giant lizard. Myra told Joey that he could see him in a way that no one else could, just him and Chris. She also told him to keep touching Chris, as he was giving her strength.

"I have come to claim you as my own. I will take you to my bed and we will be one." Joey started forward, and Chris gripped her fingers into his fur. He stayed where he was for now, but he was pissed off. "I will have you, Christiana McKenzie, and all that you have to offer."

"I offer you nothing." The monster stepped back. The venom in Chris's voice had him thinking that she was pissed too. "You will not take because you are not welcome here. You have been summoned by a lesser witch that you have killed with your anger. I have spoken."

Jackson was dead, Joey just noticed. His body had been drained. His entire head was also crushed under the weight of the monster's foot. When Tyron took another step back, Joey moved forward with Chris, but was cautioned once again to stay close to her. Once they had the monster backed up, Chris raised her free hand in the air and threw back her head.

"Lord of the underworld, I summon you to come to my aid."

Joey had no idea what she was doing, but a man dressed in a business suit and tie was standing close to them. He wasn't what he'd expected when Chris called for him, but the man bowed to her before turning to Joey.

"You are the cat, her mate and familiar?" Joey said that he was. "I owe her much for this. And you, if what you say is true."

I am all that, and a man that is in love with her.

The man nodded and turned to Tyron. He was down on one knee, his head bent almost to the ground. He looked like he was ready to meet his maker. Joey wondered what the hell was going on to Myra.

"I don't have a clue. But I'm betting that Chris does." She laughed, and he turned to look at her.

That was when he saw that his entire family had shifted to panthers, and the wolves from earlier were standing right behind them. Micah came to stand beside him and leaned into his body. It was a sign that he was there for him, as were the rest of them. Joey turned back to the under lord.

"This man, your man, sent another to claim what is not his. He has come here with the intentions of entering my home and having my mate kill himself so that he may gain my powers. I have told you what he has planned to do with them. And as you have requested, I have called to you when he stated his business."

The man nodded at Chris when she finished speaking. Then he turned to Tyron.

"You thought to use her powers against me, did you?" Tyron started to lift his head when the man spoke again. "You look at me now and I will be well within my rights to behead you. I'm not saying that it won't happen anyway, but I will kill you without your giving me your side of this…this stupidity."

"She is a lesser witch. One that is well within my rights as a powerful warlock to claim." The man looked at him, then at Chris as Tyron continued. "You know our laws as well as I do. You know what I say is true."

"What I know is that you were warned, by many I'm to understand, not to come here. You were told by the witch council that she was the grand witch. Yet here you are with a dead man stuck to the bottom of your foot like the shit that you are." Chris giggled and the man smiled at her before talking to Tyron. "Do you not remember what I said to you this afternoon when you called for my help? What did I tell you? Twice as a matter of fact."

"You said that you wash your hands of me and this folly, as she was too powerful for you to get involved with." Tyron lifted his head only enough to look at him and Chris before he spit onto the ground. "I spit in the face of your inability to see what is right before you. I did not summon you, and I have no use for your guidance."

"Oh, you misunderstand, Tyron. I'm not here for you. Well, I am, but not to help you. I'm here to take you. And I will. I'm here because this witch, the grand witch, has made me an offer that I cannot refuse. Well, that's not true either. I could, but I don't want to. She told me just what you plan to do with your magic should you take hers." Tyron looked at them again as the man laughed. "And when I'm finished with you, the council wants their part of you. If there should be anything left."

"You cannot take me anywhere. I'm a man that has no ties to you any longer." The paper appeared almost as soon as the words were out of his mouth. "What's this? My contract with you is void. You told me so when you came to take my minions with you."

"So I did, so I did. But you missed this part right here." The man held it up then snapped his fingers to make it in a more manageable form. "Let me read it to you in the event that you can't remember it. Let me see. Ah, here it is. 'Even should this contract be misrepresented by either part, there will never be any retaliation from either of the beings that have put their name to this.' That would be you and me. And since you have plotted against me, using this woman here as your powerhouse, I am well within my right to do what it says here. 'Death will be decided by the injured party.' That would be me, and you have hurt me grievously, Tyron."

With a snap of his fingers, not only was Tyron gone but the body of Jackson as well. He turned to them both, and Joey heard the low growls of his family behind him. The man stopped and put his hands up. Not that Joey trusted that any more, but he didn't move forward.

"You have what you need?" He nodded and then smiled. "I'm not going to come with you. You've asked, and I'm still telling you no."

"A man can dream, can he not?" The man bent to one knee in front of Joey and put out his hand. "I will not harm your cat, but I should like to shake your hand if you would allow it."

Chris stepped between them and the man stood up, laughing. She told him to back up before speaking again. "I think that you've overstayed your welcome, sir. It's time that you leave us alone."

"I shall. But I would like to know one thing. How did you know to summon me? I mean, of all the demons that are in my realm, how did you know to call to me?" Chris said nothing. "You're much smarter than I was led to believe, Grand Witch. If you are sure that we cannot come to some agreement, then I shall take my leave."

"I'm not going to come with you. Nor will I summon you again." He told her not to be too hasty. "I won't. Should I need help, I'll call on your boss. He was most helpful today as well."

The man stood there for several seconds before he threw back his head and laughed. When he disappeared seconds after that, Chris dropped to the ground. Joey shifted to catch her, but he was too late. She was down before he could do anything more than hold her.

~~~

Myra watched Joey and Chris. They were both sleeping soundly and had been for several hours now. She wasn't worried about them. They had no ill effects from their ordeal, but she did want to ask her about the demon. That had been a surprise to them all.

"What do you suppose she will do with a demon on her side?" Myra looked at Carol, then back at the sleeping couple. "She knew just how to take care of this and no one was hurt. Well, none of us were hurt. You think that's why she did it? To keep her family safe?"

"She's much stronger than we even knew. And to think that I came here to help her transition into this new role." Carol only snorted. "Okay, it was what I had started out wanting to do. But I think I fell in love with the two of them. Her mother would have been so proud of her."

"She would have. Had she let her do any of this in the first place. That woman was terrified of her own shadow after you talked to her. You might should have said it differently. Perhaps we might have been able to foresee this sooner." Myra said nothing. "I'm going to be staying on. I thought to leave after this was done, but if they don't care, I'm going to hang around. There are a few more of us retired old witches that need a place like this too."

"They're broke." Carol said she knew that. "I can't let them be in a situation like this. We have to make sure that they go and see where her sister put that stash. It will not get them out of debt, but it will help them along the way."

"They gotta open that thing in the barn first. Those guys that be watching it, they got themselves some families to go back to." Myra had forgotten about that. "I think I'll mention it to them when they wake. Seems only fitting that they get to it now that the trouble is all over."

"I don't think the trouble is over, do you?" Carol asked her what she meant. "There will be others, not unlike Jackson and Tyron, who will come for her. She's going to need to be on her toes and ready for anything. They won't be able to take her powers because of how strong her magic is, but they can hurt her and you."

Carol laughed and Myra turned to her. "You never did see what was right in front of your face. Did you see that family of theirs? The way them wolves, even the ones that can't be no more than they are right now, how they stood up with her and him? Hell, I'm thinking that the council would do well to get her on their side and leave the rest to her. She's a might stronger than they think, and I don't mean the magic. Those two have it all. Family, love, and more than enough heart to go around."

Myra watched them for a bit longer before she went to her own home. It was small compared to the one that she'd just left, but it suited her needs. And they were not many. She thought about what Carol had said about the couple and how they had it all. Myra had to agree with her, they did. And they'd have even more before they were to have their own children. Which by her calculations would be soon, within the next two years. And the children would have more than their parents, Myra thought.

It took her nearly three hours to get ready for the morrow. Angel had asked her just before she'd been killed to watch over her sister. It had been her dying wish that her sister have her things, and Myra was going to make sure that they got them. No matter what. In addition to the magic that she'd already taken, there were her things as well. Personal items as well as her book.

Angel had begun to write down spells that she'd found or figured out on her own. She'd been a witch that hadn't relied on her magic, but her ability to cast. Few people knew that there was a difference. But Angel had. And she'd been very good at it.

Myra knew that she had herbs too. Some that had not been around for decades, longer on some of them. Where she'd been able to find them was anyone's guess, but she had a stash of those as well. And Myra knew this and had sent Carol to the Bentley household because her knowledge of such things would bring them to life again. Then there were the gems and stones.

Most would have thought her rocks pretty bobbles to amuse. But they were more than that. They were magical. And not only that, but when put together in a certain way, they could do more harm or good than any bomb that had ever been made. Myra thought about the first time she'd seen them. And how suspicious Angel had been about her.

"Moonstone? You have moonstone? And a blue one to boot." Angel had stood in front of her case, blocking Myra from seeing them. "I won't touch them should that be what you're thinking."

"I know you won't. So just back off." Myra nodded and took a few steps back from the girl and her case of stones. "How did you find me here? I've not even registered this place as yet as my home."

"The stones called to me. I use them as well." Angel hadn't moved, nor did she speak. "I know who you are. And I knew your mother."

"So?" Myra had nodded and tried her best to hide the smile that had been fighting to come out. "If you knew her, then you knew my father. The real deal." She nodded and took another step back. The anger coming off the girl had been strong.

"I knew of him, yes. He wasn't a very good man, nor a good provider. You look like your mom. Does your sister too?"

It was all it took to have Angel on the defense. She'd been hostile before, but when Myra had brought up Chris, it was as if everything had been opened up and was raining on her. It wasn't a nice warm shower.

"You are to stay away from her. She's not what you think. Chris is stronger than any of us." Myra nodded but didn't comment. She was more concerned by the stones that came to life over Angel's head. "They belong to me."

"I can see that. You're a conjurer, aren't you? And strong too. You've called the stones to you and in turn, they've called me to you to help you." Angel had told her no. "But you know that it's true. Listen to them talk to you."

When she closed her eyes, Myra stood very still. The girl was so strong that she was draining her. When she looked at her after several moments, Myra felt as if she'd had her fingers put into an electrical outlet, her waning power surged into her just like that.

"They said that you are older than some of them." Myra nodded, not sure what the stones had said to her, but the child was smiling now. "I need for you to help me. I want...you have to know that my sister is stronger than any of us, as I have said, but something is coming for her, and I want to make sure she's prepared for it."

"She will be." Angel had nodded and lifted the small moonstone out of the case. When she put it out to her, Myra didn't even reach for it.

"It says that it belongs to you. She's missed you." Myra nodded and put out her hand. When the beautiful blue and white stone was put into her hand, Myra knew that this woman was strong too. Stronger than her. "I won't hurt you, but you'll never tell anyone, not even Chris, where I am. She might know, but she will come here and that would wake things in her that she can't have awaken yet."

"I won't tell her. But are you sure that she'll know to come here? And when she gets here, will you be able to help her?" Angel had shaken her head. "I don't understand."

"I won't be around when she comes here. And I've found a way for her to know where this is when the time is right." Myra had only nodded. "You'll see. Chris is the one that will bring magic to its knees."

~~~

The next morning, Myra was at the house when Chris and Joey came down. They had slept well, anyone could see that, but she also knew that they were at peace too. The thing in the barn would be the first thing they dealt with today, then on to the lair of Angel. It was going to take a lot out of the couple, but they were strong enough now to deal with it.

The guard that had been there since the beginning handed Joey the knife. The bands around the box had never been cut until now, and it was hard for him to get them loosened. Chris told him to use his magic, and he only stared at her. By putting her hand over his, the bands came off quickly, and then she stepped back.

The safe inside of the crate was huge, and taped to the front of it was a big envelope. Myra stayed back as the three brothers, Nolan, Bruke, and Micah, helped pull the padding away. The rest of the family had gathered as well.

Joey opened the envelope and read the contents before handing it to Chris. She looked at the pack of wolves that stood nearby. The man that stood with them was a shifter too, but he was the only one that was in human form.

"It says that you belong to him now. That he's your...." She looked at the papers in her hand before talking to the man standing there. "That Joey is your alpha. How can that be? He's a cat."

"And Emmett was a vampire, yet we served him until his death. He told me that he had picked a man to watch over us, guide us. I knew it was him and you that were our alphas when I met you in the woods." Chris asked him what he meant by her being the alpha. "As his mate, you are as much our leader as Joey is. We serve you."

The wolves lay on their backs and exposed their bellies to them. Myra told them that this was a sign of giving themselves over. Joey told her that he might have known that but thanked her. Myra watched as Joey went to the man.

"Welcome to my family, Drew."

Drew nodded and then looked at the box that had been given to him when he'd first arrived. "I cannot thank you enough for this. It was...when I asked for it, I was told that there was nothing to give me. I'm grateful for this little piece of my son."

Chris told him she wished she could have done more, but Drew backed away. It was time to open the safe.

The guard handed them the combination. If he had a name, no one had ever heard it so far as Myra knew. And the moment that Joey had it, the man as well as the other guards simply disappeared. Apparently their duty was complete now. The instructions were read on how to open it.

"Your mate, should you have one, will turn the dial first. Then you will, my friend. After that, you will turn the dial the third time, and her the last. Be aware that the door will open on its own should you do this correctly. If you have not yet found yourself a mate, then open this with your lovely mother. She will benefit anyway, but the magic will only be opened by two people who love each other very much." Joey and Chris moved to the large dial.

No one could see the numbers as the dial was moved. The ticking of it, the sound of the tumblers, was heard by them all, but no one moved to see what they were doing. As the two of them stepped back, the feeling of her magic poured from it, and she knew in that moment that the old vampire had done the impossible. He'd given all those present immortality without a single bite from him. She wondered if the old poop would let them know what he'd done to them.

There was a shield in front of whatever the safe held, and yet another envelope. Joey read it then again handed it to Chris. They were both laughing when they turned to the people with them. Joey told Chris to tell them what he'd said. Joey, she noticed, was dealing with so much pain of the loss of his friend that he'd turned his back on them again for a few moments.

"I'm going to read this to you. Some of its…well, he's going to piss a lot of you off, I think. But here goes." Chris cleared her throat. "Hello, my dearest boy. You have this because I have moved on or, sadly, I am dead. I do hope that I have gone quickly, but I think with my age and meanness that haunts me still, it will not be an easy death. I am sorry that I could not be with you during this time. But if I were, you'd have no reason to be reading this. I have given you the gift that will last a lifetime. For several of them as a matter of fact. All of you present during the opening of my gift to you will live as long as you wish. I have gifted you with immortality."

"Excuse me?" Micah stepped forward, his little girls in the stroller in front of him. "What do you mean, the gift of immortality? What if I don't want to live forever? Did he even take that into consideration?"

"I'm not sure what he took into consideration. But you have it to deal with it." Joey took the letter from Chris and continued reading. "I have left you this to keep you in a lifestyle that I hope you will enjoy. I started to save my money when I first was turned, in the event that someday I might buy myself an island and live there. The money that you will see in this is what I might have spent on food had I needed it, power of light when it became available and I never used, and also the cars that I didn't purchase, the gas I never used, and the tires that I had no use for. This, I leave for you and yours."

Joey went back to the safe and pulled down the protective covering. Inside it were small envelopes, large ones too. Bags of gems and other jewels. There were deeds to properties all over the world.

"How much?" Joey turned to Myra and asked the question again. "You know, don't you? How much is this worth?"

But she didn't answer him. Chris did. And when she told him, even Micah was amazed. There was more in this one safe than all the money in all the banks in this state alone. There were billions upon billions worth of cash and jewels. Not counting the property, she told him, they were set for the rest of their lives and then some.

"What the hell am I supposed to do with all this? I mean, this is more...this is just too much." Chris nodded and told him they'd be able to help so many, and that was when Myra took her leave of them. They were going to be just fine, the lot of them.

Chapter 15

The trip to the warehouse near the house where she'd lived wasn't long. She was nervous about it, still hating to fly, but with Joey next to her, it wasn't nearly as bad as she'd thought it would be. As soon as they were in the air, he dismissed the staff and took off his seat belt.

"I'm going to show you how to fly." Chris thought for sure he was going to take her to the cockpit, and there was no way that was going to happen. But when he sat down on his knees in front of her and pulled her to the edge of the seat, she felt her body respond to his nearness. "We can do this here or in the bedroom in the back. I'd rather be in here, but it's up to you."

"What are you going to do to me?" His grin had her panties soaked. "Someone could see us. We can't do this now."

"Oh, but we can. And we will. Try not to scream too much. We don't want the pilot to come and see what we're about." Her skirt was pulled up over her hips with her help. Then he ran his hand up under her blouse. "I'm going to eat you. And when I'm done, I'm going to fuck you right here on this floor."

Her legs were pulled open, and he slid his finger into her. She was riding his hand, feeling her body heat up, when he leaned into her ear and told her that when she came, he was going to bite her on the leg.

"Yes, please." Joey moved so that his mouth was only inches from her pussy, and she raised her hips up for him. His soft chuckle had her curling her fingers into his hair and pulling him to her. She needed him right now.

As soon as his warm breath touched against her exposed clit, she cried out, and then he sucked her into his mouth, and she came twice before he lifted his head and looked at her.

"I'm not finished, but I need you on the floor. I want you to come with my cat fucking you with his tongue." She was on the floor before she could tell him she wasn't sure this was the place for that. And when he shifted, his large cat stilling between her open thighs, she nearly screamed when he lapped at her clit hard, his tongue pressing against her until she thought she was going to pass out, the pleasure was so great.

His tongue entered her, seemed to touch her in places that set her heart to racing and her wanting more. But each time she was close, her body ready to explode, he moved to her clit again and a new pleasure was hers. Chris was begging him to end her torment by then, her body covered in a sheen of sweat that made her hands sliding over her bare breasts feel wonderful. Her nipples ached to be sucked, and tugging on them didn't give her what she needed. Finally she commanded him to take her, to give her what she needed.

The lick along her thigh had her crying out, not from pain but pure pleasure. And when his teeth sank into her, biting her hard enough that she thought she'd be sick from it, he lifted his head just when she was going to tell him it was enough. His shift from cat to man was flawless. He entered her in one fluid motion. Then he stilled above her.

"You're in heat." Chris had no idea what that meant so asked him. "You can have a child if we wish it…if you wish it."

"Now? I mean, you can know that?" He nodded and her body responded to his slow moment inside of her. "Please, stop and tell me what you want."

"You. I want you right now. And I want to see you swollen with our child." He moved again, bringing a shiver of need over her. "If I come in you right now, there's a good chance that you'll conceive. If I stop now, then we can wait until the next cycle."

He moved again, and his cock seemed to swell inside of her. Her mind wanted him to slow down, to think this through, but her body, the master of her it seemed at the moment, told her to shut the hell up and let him fill her. Wrapping her feet over his thighs, riding upward when he moved down, she told him to fill her. Give her a child.

He pounded her hard now. His cock seemed to fill even more, and her body, ready to receive him, seemed to open wider, tighten around him as if needing to take all of him into her. When he took her breast into his mouth and chewed on just the hard peak, she held him, knowing that she was going to fly away as soon as she came.

When her release came, it was as if everything within her and around them paused. The air that moved around them, the small specks of dust in the air floated slower, even the breath she held, her heart beats, all of it seemed to have been waiting for the moment that he came and brought her with him. And then it happened. They were tossed over the edge of their mutual release in the exact moment, and she knew that a child was there. Joey gave her what no other would ever give her, the gift of another life.

As Joey dropped on her, Chris closed her eyes. It was too much. All the colors in the room seemed to have brightened to a degree that her eyes hurt. Every sound in the tiny room, from Joey's breathing to her own beating heart, seemed to have amplified in that moment. And when he lifted his head and looked down at her, Chris knew the true meaning of the world love.

"I love you." He kissed her gently on the mouth with a hunger that she knew was love. And when he lifted his head from her this time, he rolled them to his back, taking her with him. Chris thought she could sleep this way for the rest of her days.

"I love you very much. I want you to know that I really do want a child with you. I should have asked you before I was inside of you." Chris smiled at him and told him he wasn't getting off that easy. "Yeah, I didn't think so. But I promise to make it up to you. If we didn't make a baby right now, when we get to the hotel, we'll try again. Harder."

The pilot said they were twenty minutes from landing. Joey gathered their clothing, and as they dressed he asked her what she thought they'd find where they were going. She told him she had no idea.

"I've not even thought of the place in years. Angel and I used to go there, this big warehouse, when we got out of school. At first it was a way to get away from our dad. He wasn't abusive to us, but he was to Mom. While she worked, we'd go there and play. Sometimes coming home after she was already there." She grinned then. "I think she knew what we were doing, staying away until she was there. We just didn't care for our father at all."

"And your sister wanted you to go there and find whatever it was she left you. Do you think it'll still be there after all this time?" Chris had no idea why, but she felt that her sister would have put it out in plain sight for her and no one else. She told Joey this. "So she would have used magic to hide it for you."

"Yes. Angel was...she was very powerful. I think, and I know that this sounds crazy, but I think she was always trying to protect me. Not just when we were together, but even when we were separated. I could feel her there, guiding me in the right direction when I seemed lost."

Joey nodded. "My dad too. Whenever I feel like I'm going to fuck up, I can hear his voice telling me to stop listening to whoever was trying to get me into a mess and listen to my head. It was always right." They were seated when he continued. "You would have loved him. And he would have been over the moon with you and Reggie."

"I wish I could have known him. But your mom swears that all I need to do is look at the six of you and there he is. Not in looks so much, she said, but in personality and the way you guys work. She said that Micah looks the most like him, but the rest of you have traits of him as well."

They landed a few minutes later. It had been so long it seemed since she'd been here, when it had only been a month and a half. So much had changed in that time and it was all for the good. As the limo took them to their destination, she thought of the time when Angel had told her about the place.

"It calls to me. I'm going to own it someday too." Angel had been all of ten and Chris, nine when she'd said that.

"And when I own it, I'm going to make it into a magical place where children can come and play. No big people would be allowed."

"How will the kids get here if not for the big people?" Angel told her she didn't know but they'd know to come there.

Chris decided to make such a place when they got home. Maybe not where the adults couldn't come in, but it would be a place where children, sick children, could think of it as being magical. And to some it would be. She asked Joey about it.

"I think it's a wonderful idea. I know that there are some empty houses near the downtown area. Not far from the hospital as a matter of fact." The car came to a smooth stop. "Are you ready for this?"

"Yes. No. I'm not sure." He didn't push her, which she was grateful for. "What could she have left me? I only wish she was here. That would be all I ever needed."

"Let's go and see. If it's something too painful for you, then we'll just leave. As you said, there is very little else she can leave you other than her being here." Joey moved to the door, and she slid out with him.

~~~

Joey wanted to shelter her from any more pain. It had been a hard few months for her, and he was worried that this wasn't going to help. Allen was going to be back in a few days. He'd been working on finishing up his mom's estate with the new will. He'd decided to stay in her home, for now he'd told them. Just to give the two of them some privacy. Joey thought the man felt a little left out, what with his overly loud family. They would make sure he felt welcome when he came back.

The building looked like any other warehouse that he'd seen. There were broken windows on the lower level and a few on the upper ones. But what really surprised him was the new roof. But when he touched the door to open it, the entire building changed.

"Her magic." Joey nodded, thinking that if she could do this and be a lesser witch than her sister, he was going to be a little concerned when Chris came into her own. "She's made it so that you can only see what she wants you to see. The windows aren't broken in this view, and the walls are painted. How much you want to bet that Myra helped with the paint job?"

It looked like someone had gotten a great deal on some very bright and colorful paint but didn't really plan on how it was to go on the building. Or maybe they had. It looked like they'd taken the cans of paint and simply dropped them from a helicopter. But instead of looking gaudy or weird, it suited the big building. As soon as they moved into the building, he could see more of her magic.

She had made her place for children.

There was color in here too, but it was more balanced, there were great paintings of animals in play, balloons that were in flight, as well as butterflies. The colors were bright, happy, and would make even the most ill child smile. He walked around with Chris, holding her hand as she pointed out different things that caught her eye.

Hanging from the roof above them were streamers and stars and other things dangling from wires. Well above his head, he could see that time had been taken with each one, so that no one would be harmed by them. There were large areas covered with rugs and pillows partitioned off with folding walls. Everywhere you looked there were shelves with books on them. And stuffed animals of every kind lying atop them. In the center of the room was a table; it had a light hanging down so that it shone on a laptop. They made their way to this.

Chris sat down at the chair and then booted up the computer. As they waited, Joey looked around. He realized then what this place was.

"It's being used." Chris nodded. "I wonder how long she's had this going. I mean, someone is watching it for her. So I wonder how long she's had this up and running."

The computer started up, and a small sticky note told them where to go. The password was Angel's middle name. After Chris typed in the word Carolyn, the computer came to life. There was a video to run, and they both could see who Chris said was her sister. Chris pressed the enter key so that it would begin.

"I've had this set up in the event that I'm killed. I know that going to work for these people will be dangerous, but things must go in the order that has been set before you can be what you are. You see, I've been able to see what you will become, and I wanted to tell you how very proud of you I am." There was a slight pause, and Angel smiled. "I don't want to die. I...I'm such a sap. Hang on."

The video was paused, and then it moved again. Angel was in a different shirt, and the room she was in was darker now, as if some time had passed. She smiled again before beginning.

"Okay, no more talk about dying today. I've eighty-five people helping with this project that you're currently standing in. They come in daily and set up the kitchen that will feed the children breakfast and then again for lunch. We don't have the funds yet to supply dinner but.... Anyway. We have over a hundred kids that come in for play time here. They can do what they want and the place is safeguarded against anyone that will try to harm them. You'd be surprised how many people have been turned away by the magic because of their true self." She looked away, then looked into the camera again. "I'd ask that you try to keep this up and running for them. I have some things for you to sell if your funding doesn't cover this. They're my little stones. Myra will buy some of them. She's expressed a desire to have the moonstones. There are any number of people that will want some of them as well. Then there are the ones that I have made just for you."

The camera panned to a large table, and even before the camera focused on them and not Angel any longer, he could see that there was a great many of them. Angel picked one of them up before continuing.

"This is a moonstone that has been enhanced. I got to be pretty good at it and would make them magical to only the person who holds them. Anyone else…well, they're just pretty rocks. There is a number on the back of each of them. If you could see if the person still wants them, their names are in this book here." The book was shown, then it was put into the drawer beneath the table. "If you can't do this, that's fine too. I know that you and that husband of yours will be extremely happy and will live a very long time. I helped Emmett work his magic to give to you as well. I'm not sure what plans he had for it, but there you have it."

The camera paused again, and Angel was in front of it again. This time she'd been crying again, and Chris gripped his hand tighter.

"Now for the shitty part. Tell Dad that I loved him. Very much. He encouraged me when no one else, other than you, would. He kept me sane, too, when I started having the visions. He never knew about them, but he did know that I'd been upset. Keep him close to you, please." A tissue was handed to her, and she thanked someone off camera. "Chris, I will miss you daily, if not every minute of my afterlife. You were my role model in your strength and focus. I am all I am because of you. Please be happy for me. I need to know that you will be. And if you have a mind to, name one of those beautiful babies you're going to have after me. Not Angel, that's a hard name to live up to. And as you know, I went in the opposite direction with that one. But Carolyn would be awesome. I will watch over you and try to keep you safe."

Chris was sobbing when Angel broke down. Joey had to look away too. It was hard knowing that this woman knew her death was coming and had stopped to reassure her sister. When Angel cleared her throat, they both looked again.

"Joseph Bentley. Yeah, I know about you too. There is so much I could tell you. I could threaten you too, but I won't. You're a good man and will make my sister very happy. Or else." Her laughter bubbled out. "Your family is...will always be there for the two of you. And when you least expect it, things will look brighter than you've ever imagined. Oh. I almost forgot. Your brother—I'm sorry, I don't know his name, as I only know faces—but your brother the doctor is having some major issues right now. He's broke. I mean, he's going to move back home and give up his car because he can no longer afford it broke. But all for a good cause. Had I met him before all this, we would have made a good team. His help to the homeless in your town will help so many people if he gets some help. If he asks for help. Are all you Bentley men stubborn?"

"Yes." Joey kissed Chris on the cheek when she answered her sister. The video stopped at that point and neither of them moved. When Chris looked at him, he knew what she was going to say. "I don't want to sell her things. Do you think I could make enough money to keep this place running as well as helping out your brother?"

"We can help them both. We will help them both." She nodded and then they turned when someone called out hello. After spending two hours with Debra Jenkins, they left for their hotel.

Joey was excited to start this new part of his life. The Children's Place was not just going to be a safe haven here, but where they were too. And after making a few calls, he found that not only was Nolan broke, he was indeed having to move home. The first thing they were going to do when they got back was sit him down and have a long talk about family. Joey was excited about that as well. The Bentleys were kicking ass and taking names, as of right now.

Now Available, book one of the Bentley Legacy, *Micah*

Micah Bentley is a third generation cop and a panther. He always wanted to be a homicide detective like his dad, but kept getting passed up for the job because he was too good at what he currently did working the beat. Micah has a gift, he can read people's minds. Such a gift could be a help and a hindrance on a job. He could pluck the information he needs right out of someone's mind, but knowing they're guilty and proving it are two different things. But when his dad is killed off duty it has him rethinking his career choice.

Regina Webster, Reggie to her friends, is just trying to make ends meet by working three jobs to keep her head above water, and also take care of her invalid brother. She doesn't have time for socializing with bossy men like Micah Bentley who butt into her life making everything concerning her his business. She doesn't know anything about this mate thing he keeps spouting off about, she just wants him to leave her alone.

Due to a random act of violence, she finds herself suddenly homeless: no home, no money, no car and suffering from a gunshot wound to boot. Reggie has no choice but to accept a helping hand from the Bentleys at least until she can get back on her feet.

Trouble has Reggie marked, and this time they take Micah's mom too. Micah knows they're in trouble, but when the bad guys don't go where they're expected it's a race against the clock…

Before You Go...

Share your voice and help guide other readers to Kathi Barton's wonderful books. Even if it's only a line or two your reviews help readers discover Kathi's books so that she can continue creating stories that you'll love. Login to your favorite retailer and leave a review.

AWARD WINNING, BESTSELLING AUTHOR

Kathi Barton, author of the bestselling series Force of Nature, lives in Nashport, Ohio with her husband Paul. In addition to writing full time Kathi likes to spend time with her eight grandkids, three children and three children-in-laws. She writes to relax and have fun.

Her muse, a cross between Jimmy Stewart and Hugh Jackman brings them to life for her readers in a way that has them coming back time and again for more. Her favorite genre is paranormal romance with a great deal of spice. You can visit Kathi on line and drop her an email if you'd like. She loves hearing from her fans. aaronskiss@gmail.com.

Follow Kathi on her blog:
http://kathisbartonauthor.blogspot.com/

www.ingramcontent.com/pod-product-compliance
Lightning Source LLC
Chambersburg PA
CBHW032123170626
46808CB00006B/2088